THE FRUIT GUM MURDERS

An enthralling crime mystery full of twists

ROGER SILVERWOOD

Yorkshire Murder Mysteries Book 21

JOFFE BOOKS

Revised edition 2020
Joffe Books, London
www.joffebooks.com

First published in Great Britain in 2014

ISBN: 978-1-78931-597-4

ONE

223 Canal Road, Bromersley, South Yorkshire
June 2007

Lydia Tinker loved men. And men adored Lydia. From a baby she had cooed and giggled and squealed with delight much more when in her father's arms than when in her mother's. When she was five, her father bought her a beautiful rocking horse that she treasured and she was always on its red plastic saddle rocking away.

At six she had always been eager to play postman's knock, so that she could kiss the boys. At ten, she had set her sights on teenage boys, but they had tended to ignore her. Her age and her size were not in her favour, even though, so young, she did have golden curly hair and a dimple in her cheek.

At fifteen — she had looked nearer twenty — she had caught the eye of a boy of fourteen called Cedric, a podgy, lonely, awkward lad who had minimal knowledge of algebra, knew nothing of the wives of Henry VIII and thought that Pythagoras's theorem had something to do with a hippopotamus. Cedric made up for his ignorance of academic subjects by his experience and knowledge of more worldly and mature subjects. Encouraged by Lydia, they forged an enthusiastic relationship, eager to learn, explore and experiment.

So by the time Lydia was eighteen, she had fallen in and out of promiscuous relationships with boys, and then men, almost as often as a police camera caught a speeding young driver on the Barnsley ring road. Cedric was history. And Lydia's collection of gold rings rivalled that of H. Samuel.

She adored jewellery; rings with big shiny diamonds, antique gold pendants with delicate seed pearls, peridots and garnets, pearls of all sizes and colours, emeralds, rubies, gold earrings of absolutely every style, gold chains — the more they glittered, the heavier they were and the more they rattled, the more she adored them. At police functions, she always looked stunning and wore the most beautiful dresses and jewellery, easily outshining the Chief Constable's wife on all fronts.

Lydia lived with her mother and younger sister, Nadine, in a tiny two-up and two-down terraced house on Canal Street, a less than salubrious district of Bromersley.

Nadine was a bit plumper than her streamlined sister, Lydia. She had the pitted remains of acne on her face. Also Nadine won no prizes academically. Her schoolwork reports upset her mother; her reading was bad and her writing worse. She could identify coins and paper money, but was hopeless at shopping. Her mother was so embarrassed at times that she told people that Nadine was dyslexic.

That June night, while Nadine, 17, was in the tiny kitchen on the sofa playing 'Find the Dragon' on her laptop, and their mother, Maureen, was washing up the tea pots at the sink, Lydia came down the stairs wearing a new yellow dress which was very striking.

'Do you like this, Mum?' she said, running a hand down her stomach to straighten any creases there might have been.

Her mother had a cigarette in the corner of her mouth. She stopped pushing the pots around in the sink and turned round. She looked admiringly at the dress. Then her face changed. She was not pleased.

Lydia looked into her mother's eyes and giggled.

'I know what I'm doing, Mum, honestly,' Lydia said. 'Anyway, what do you think to the *dress*?'

Nadine looked up from the sofa. 'I think it's fab. Can I borrow it next Saturday?'

'Won't fit *you*,' Lydia said. 'Besides you'd pull the catches.'

Nadine pulled a face and called out, 'Meanie!'

'I just want you to find a decent man and be happy,' Maureen Tinker said.

'What about me?' Nadine said.

'You as well. You know that. Bringing you two up proper is damned hard work.'

'Who's complaining?' Lydia said.

'Yeah,' Nadine said. 'Who's complaining?'

'Well . . . I suppose I am. It's not been easy, you know. Your father gone, Nadine's father is still in Armley. It worries me, on my own, trying to keep you two on the straight and narrow.'

'You don't regret having me and Nadine, do you?' Lydia said.

'What's brought all this on?' Nadine said.

'I didn't expect to have to bring you both up on my own,' Maureen said. Then her face changed. A small smile changed into a big smile. 'You daft cat,' she said. She turned away from the sink, wiped her hands on a tea towel, grabbed Lydia's arms tightly, looked into her eyes and said, 'I just don't want you to finish up like *me*. You've got the most beautiful face in the world, and what's more important, a lovely nature. Whatever man gets you will be the luckiest man in the world.'

Lydia pulled away. 'Don't worry about me, Mum. You want me to enjoy myself, don't you?'

' 'Course I do,' Maureen said as she turned back to the sink, picked up the dishcloth, and putting her hands into the water, pulled out a plate.

'*You* could go out, you know,' Lydia said. 'You could soon get a bloke. Just about every man on this street looks at you . . . in that way . . . when you go out.'

Nadine looked up.

Maureen blinked. 'Huh! In what way?' she said and shook her head. 'I don't think so. It's you they're looking at.'

'You're not past it yet, Mum. I've seen them from the front-room window . . . looking after you.'

'They're just a street full of old lechers. Don't fancy any of them. Can't go out, anyway. Not while I've got this . . . this chest.'

She coughed. She made the low note of a foghorn.

She had been smoking since she was twelve. Smoking cheap cigarettes for forty years was beginning to take its toll on her.

Lydia waved her arms in the air impatiently. 'Anyway, you still haven't said what you think to the dress, Mum. It's out of the catalogue. Four pounds a week.'

Maureen turned back to the sink. 'If you can afford it. What you do with your money is nothing to do with me. I've got these pots to do.'

Lydia's eyes flashed. 'Look at it, Mum. What do you think?'

Maureen banged down a cup on the draining board, turned and said, 'If you must know, Lydia, it's a tart's dress. It's too short, too tight, frames your backside and shows too much cleavage.'

Lydia forced a smile. 'I knew you'd like it.'

Nadine looked up from the sofa and said, 'I think it's really lovely, Lydia. I want one just like it.'

Maureen glared at Nadine and said, 'You're not wearing anything as vulgar as *that*.'

Nadine pulled a disagreeable face and turned back to the laptop.

Maureen threw the dishcloth into the bowl, put her hands on her hips and slowly shook her head. Eventually she said, 'You know, love, you really will have to be careful. You've fooled around with men and got your own way with them all your life. One day, you will push your luck once too often, and you will get hurt, or up the duff, or both.'

'Don't worry. All the men I meet are gentlemen, *real* gentlemen, Mum.' She giggled again.

Maureen lifted her eyes to the ceiling. 'Huh. Different bloke every night.' She turned back to the sink.

Lydia snatched up her sequin-covered purse from the table and pulled open the back door.

Maureen wrinkled up her nose. The muscles in her lips tightened.

'Have a nice time,' she said, then in a hard, stern voice she added, 'but be in by 10.30.'

Lydia's eyes flashed. 'Don't wait up,' she snapped.

Maureen was furious. 'I don't want any lip from you!' she called and she threw the first thing to hand, which was a pan that had been drying on the draining board.

But Lydia was too quick. She was already outside. She quickly slammed the door.

'You tart!' Maureen yelled. 'You bloody tart!' Her heart was pounding, and she began to cough. She coughed and coughed for more than five minutes. Nadine came rushing up to her with a box of tissues.

Two years later, in February 2009, Maureen Tinker died unexpectedly. Lydia and Nadine were distraught for some months, especially Nadine, who was also particularly low because she had left school and had been unable to get a job. After a few false starts, Lydia managed to get her a rather lowly job as a nursing assistant at a care home on the outskirts of town. Nadine was very nervous at the beginning, but after a few weeks, as she got to know the other staff and the patients, she began to look forward to it. She particularly liked the white coat and white hat she had to wear, which she thought made her look important.

Meanwhile, Lydia drifted in and out of a relationship with a new boyfriend, Stewart Twelvetrees, a handsome young man who was a newly qualified solicitor in the town. He was the only son of the barrister, Marcus Twelvetrees, who was head of chambers at the Crown Prosecution Service in Bromersley. Then one day, after a tempestuous courtship,

Stewart Twelvetrees put the question to Lydia, who eventually agreed and they were married in June 2009. They set up home in a small old country house on the outskirts of Bromersley. It was known as the Brambles, Old Horse Lane, Bromersley. Nadine came to live with them.

Lydia settled down to married life very quickly and soon began to buy small antiques and paintings. She and Stewart were very happy. Regrettably, apart from clothes, the only other item good enough to be brought from the old house on Canal Road was the rocking horse she had played with as a child. She said it was her greatest treasure and the only happy remembrance from her childhood. Stewart said that it would be a useful toy when they had children of their own. It took pride of place halfway up the old stairs, where there was space on a step at the turn.

Muick Castle, Bromersley, South Yorkshire
Saturday, 1 June 2013

Four years later, Lydia and Stewart Twelvetrees and Nadine Tinker were invited to a very posh ball in aid of cancer research, sponsored by Mrs Nancy Mackenzie. It was held in Muick Castle by kind permission of Lady Muick. The castle was not very old and was a fake really, built around 1850 at the whim of the late Lord Muick's great-great-grandfather, to his own specification.

The ball was a black-tie occasion and anybody who was anybody in Bromersley was there, dressed in their finery.

Detective Inspector Michael Angel and his wife were there, the serene Mary looking ravishing and extremely fashionable, her husband looking less composed. He may have been one of the handsome men there, but smiles from him were limited. He kept running his hand round the inside rim of his collar, pulling at it and muttering.

'Leave it alone,' Mary kept saying out of the side of her mouth.

'What time do we eat?' he said.

Angel was totally against dressing up for dinner-suit events like this, and was only persuaded by Mary to accompany her as she was on this particular charity committee.

In the big, oval-shaped hall, there were lots of small tables and chairs arranged near the walls, to leave the centre of the hall for dancing. At the bottom of the grand staircase on a raised dais sat Mrs Nancy Mackenzie. She was the leading light in Bromersley, seemingly in charge of all charities and all good works. She had sponsored the evening and organized everything and everybody. Next to her was Lady Muick, a pleasant looking lady wearing a most striking diamond and emerald necklace. On her right was Sir Rodney Stamp, a stiff looking man with a fierce face and tiny black eyes. He was holding a glass of claret. A young man in tails appeared from time to time with a fresh glass, which was quickly exchanged without comment. Next to Sir Rodney Stamp was a pretty young woman half his age, with a big bosom, long legs, and wearing a glittering gold dress the length of a T-shirt.

At the other end of the room was a six-piece orchestra, playing 'Blue Danube', and a few bold couples over fifty were dancing on the big space in the centre of the hall.

The hall was filling up and the dance floor was becoming busier.

Mary Angel turned to her husband and said, 'Well, are you going to ask me to dance or not?'

Angel's face creased. Then he listened to the music.

Mary said, 'It's all right. It's a waltz. You can do a waltz.'

'I know. I know.'

After a few moments, he stood up, bowed slightly and said, 'Would you care to have this dance with me, madam?'

'Thank you, kind sir,' she replied and they sailed off into the middle of the room.

Angel concentrated on the steps carefully. He could manage the waltz but that was all. He directed Mary and himself to the far side of the dance floor and then made a course around the edge of the dancing area to see who was there that he knew. When he got used to the footwork, he said, by way of making conversation, 'Did Nancy Mackenzie sell all the tickets?'

'She could have sold more, but she decided that 600 was as many as the place would hold.'

He nodded. 'That seems a tall order. Mind you, the place is pretty big.' They reached the far side and he started their journey round the perimeter.

'Let's hope that not everybody wants to dance at the same time,' Mary said. 'Nice orchestra, if it's not pretentious to call a sextet an orchestra,' she added.

Angel suddenly smiled at somebody and mouthed, 'Good evening.'

Mary said, 'Who was that?'

'Young Twelvetrees and his wife. Lydia and Stewart. They make a beautiful couple.'

He swung Mary round so that she was facing them.

'Which are they?' she said.

'Sitting. Against the wall. She's wearing a fluffy white dress and a big pendant of pearls and some other stones.'

'Sapphires,' Mary said. 'Oh yes, she's very attractive. So is he. Handsome like his father. Who is the girl standing next to Lydia Twelvetrees?'

'Lydia's sister, Nadine.'

'Her sister? They don't look like sisters.'

'No. I think Nadine is handicapped, mentally.'

'I didn't know. Poor lass ... that necklace is a bit vulgar, though.'

'What necklace? Oh the one Lydia's wearing? It's not vulgar. You always say that if a piece of jewellery is big.'

'Jewellery should be discreet . . . delicate.'

'You mean cheap . . . have you seen what Lady Muick is wearing?'

'Well, she can wear *anything*. She's got the presence.'

'You mean because she's a big lump?'

They made a few more turns and finished up where they started.

Mary's face straightened and she shook her head.

'That emerald and diamond piece round her neck must be worth around a hundred thousand pounds,' Angel said.

Mary's eyebrows shot up. 'As much as that?'

The 'Blue Danube' music came to an end. Mary and Michael Angel stopped dancing, as did all the others. They applauded the orchestra and took their seats.

Michael put his fingers down inside his collar again and began pulling it.

Mary saw him and looked round to see if he was being observed. 'Don't do that,' she said.

'It's sticking in, Mary. It's uncomfortable.'

'You will insist on wearing your father's old dress collars. If you would let me get some—'

'There's too much starch on the damned thing.'

'There isn't any starch on it at all. Starch went out in the Dark Ages. I'll get you a couple of new collars . . .'

Suddenly, there was a loud roll on the drums and a crash of cymbals. The lights went out and a spotlight showed up a young man in front of the sextet.

The Great Hall went silent and everybody stared in the direction of the stage.

'Good evening, ladies and gentlemen, and welcome to the charity ball in the Great Hall here in Muick Castle, graciously permitted by Lady Muick and sponsored by Mrs Nancy Mackenzie. I am your MC for the evening.'

The MC was abruptly interrupted by a loud scream from the opposite end of the Great Hall.

In the dark, everybody turned towards the disturbance.

A voice called out, 'Put the lights on.' Several others repeated the suggestion.

The lights went up.

It was Lady Muick. She was on her feet, her face white, her eyes staring, her fingers feeling round her long, scraggy neck. 'My necklace! My necklace! It's gone. It's gone.'

Sir Rodney Stamp leaned over to her and said, 'Where did you have it last?'

Lady Muick eyed him with huge eyes and said, 'Round my neck. It's been taken in the dark.'

He blinked, took a gulp out of his glass. The young woman next to him grabbed him by the arm and whispered something.

The crowd began to mutter among themselves.

Mrs Nancy Mackenzie got to her feet and in a slow and confident voice said, 'Ladies and gentlemen.'

The muttering stopped.

'Ladies and gentlemen,' she continued, 'would you please look around you and see if you can see an emerald and diamond necklace? It's very beautiful . . . and unmistakable. It belongs to Lady Muick. If anybody knows anything about it, please come and tell me quickly. I'm sure it will turn up. Then we can return to having a most wonderfully enjoyable evening. Thank you. Thank you very much.' Then she added, 'Mr MC, would you please ask the gentlemen of the orchestra to play some music? Thank you.'

Mrs Mackenzie then looked at Lady Muick. She was feverishly searching through her handbag. Her hands were shaking. Mrs Mackenzie crossed to her and whispered something, to which her ladyship replied. Then Mrs Mackenzie dipped into her own bag and found a pen and a small notepad.

The microphone boomed out, 'Please take your partners for a quickstep.'

The orchestra began to play 'In the mood'. The floor soon filled up with dancers.

Mary turned to her husband said, 'Isn't it awful, Michael?'

He nodded. He was thinking.

Then she said, 'Can't you offer to do something?'

'Like what?'

'Well, you're a policeman, aren't you?'

'As far as I know, I'm the only one here.'

'Well, you could *offer*,' she said.

'There's a limit on what I can do on my own, Mary,' he said.

The young footman who had been replenishing Sir Rodney Stamp's glass appeared, leaned over the table and quietly said, 'Excuse me, sir. Detective Inspector Angel?'

'Yes, lad, what is it?'

'I have a note for you from Mrs Mackenzie.'

Angel unfolded the small piece of paper. In immaculate writing he read, 'Inspector Angel, would you be kind enough to meet me in Lady Muick's sitting room. The footman will accompany you. Thank you. Nancy Mackenzie.'

'Of course,' Angel said to the footman, and he passed the note on to Mary. 'Won't be long,' he said.

Then he stood up. 'I'll follow you, lad. Lead the way.'

Mary looked gently into his eyes and said, 'Do what you can, love.'

'Of course,' he said.

Then the footman walked as quickly as he could, weaving between people standing, sitting, talking or dancing, across the bottom of the staircase where now only Sir Rodney Stamp and his escort were seated. With Angel still following him, he made his way out of the Great Hall into the huge dining room and then through that to a door, where he knocked and waited a moment or two. It was opened by Mrs Nancy Mackenzie.

TWO

Nancy Mackenzie smiled, which was unusual. Angel thought she couldn't smile.

'Ah, Inspector, come in. Thank you for coming,' she said. She had a strong voice and spoke as if she was addressing a political meeting of deaf halfwits.

Angel noticed a strong smell of brandy.

At the far end of the room, he saw Lady Muick sitting in an upholstered chair. She looked very pale and was fidgeting, sometimes looking at and fondling a tumbler that had a drop of something alcoholic, probably brandy in it. That would explain the smell. Standing by her side, erect and with his shoulders back, was a large man in a morning coat, and black-and-grey-striped trousers.

'Sit down there, Inspector,' Mrs Mackenzie said.

'What can I do for you?' Angel said.

'That is, of course, her ladyship and the man there is her butler,' she said.

Angel nodded politely towards her ladyship, who waved a shaking hand and bowed her head slightly to one side.

Mrs Mackenzie sat down close beside him. 'Now, you can see what a pickle her ladyship is in, Inspector. She tells me that the emeralds are twelve matching stones from South

America, that the necklace is worth more than a hundred thousand pounds and that it's a family piece. What are we to do?'

Angel's mind was in overdrive. 'Short of asking all the guests if they know anything about it, and searching the premises, very little.'

'We must do that, then. But surely we can do more?'

Angel looked at her and shook his head. 'Mrs Mackenzie, *everybody* is a suspect. The castle would need sealing off, and I *mean* sealing off, and everybody would need to be searched and interviewed. And every nook and cranny, receptacle, pot and pan, drain and ledge checked. I couldn't do that on my own. And if the necklace has been stolen by professional thieves, it will be miles away from here already.'

'Oh no, oh no,' Lady Muick said. Obviously, she could hear every word.

'Can you tell me what time the necklace went missing, Mrs Mackenzie?'

'Ask her yourself, Inspector.'

'I heard you,' Lady Muick said. 'It was when the lights went out. I don't quite know what it was, but the light going out made me think about my personal safety and security, and I felt round my neck for my necklace and discovered that it wasn't there.'

Mrs Mackenzie said, 'That's about ten or twelve minutes ago, now.'

'You didn't feel it go, ma'am?' Angel said.

'No. I didn't feel anything.'

Angel said, 'We would have needed a squad of men here already if we had expected a job like this. And a warrant to detain people and search them.'

Her ladyship said, 'I wouldn't want everybody searching . . . like common criminals, Inspector. Many of these good people are my friends and well known to me. Whatever would they think?'

Angel said, 'It's not practical under these particular circumstances anyway, your ladyship. So don't worry, we won't be doing any such thing unless we have evidence that they may know something.'

He turned back to Mrs Mackenzie. 'I can ring the station and have them send out as many men as they can muster, probably eight or ten constables at this time, but we could not properly organize a watertight search and rescue unit to find the necklace at such short notice.'

'I'm a JP,' Mrs Mackenzie said. 'I can sign any warrant you might need.'

'I know that, Mrs Mackenzie, but I would still have to go to the station and get the warrant itself and write it up. Meanwhile another hundred people could have left the castle.'

'I see what you mean,' she said. 'Right, well, what *can* we do?'

'I can go round the hall and ask everybody one by one if they know anything at all about the necklace. If they say no, there's nothing I can do about it. Then you could have the staff — how many staff are there engaged for this ball?'

'Forty-two. They are mostly ex-employees, known to her ladyship or me. About a dozen more volunteered for the work and were personally vetted by me.'

'Well,' Angel said, 'perhaps you could ask each of them individually if they know anything about the necklace?'

'Indeed, I can and I will.'

'Then organize them to search around the castle systematically. Every room, box, packet, place, ledge, drawer . . .'

'I can do that as well,' Mrs Mackenzie said, eager to get on with it. 'Can we do anything when the patrons are leaving?'

'Only wait at the door, to give the witness, the thief or the finder the chance to speak up. It also shows that we are on the lookout . . . that we are alert. I haven't much faith that any of these measures will necessarily recover the necklace if it has been deliberately stolen, but under the circumstances these are the only steps we can take at this stage.'

'Well, thank you, Inspector.'

He reached into his pocket for his mobile. 'I'll phone the station and get the men out.'

At Bromersley Police Station, the duty sergeant directed men who were on duty in the station and those out on routine property-checking procedures to Muick Castle. Then Angel began his personal excursion round the Great Hall, asking if anyone had seen the necklace or knew anything at all about it being missing.

DS Clifton, the night duty control sergeant, managed to assemble twelve uniformed men, who arrived around fifteen minutes later. There was one main entrance to the castle through the big door, a rear door to the stables and gardens, a kitchen door, and the French windows in the larger drawing room. Angel quickly briefed them and directed them to their posts, instructing them to stay near the actual door itself so that everyone leaving would have to pass very close to a uniformed man or woman.

Angel continued his personal journey round the Great Hall. He reached Sir Rodney Stamp and his young lady. He stepped up onto the dais and said, 'Excuse me, have either of you seen anything of Lady Muick's necklace?'

The man glared at him as if Angel had accused him of picking his nose. 'How *dare* you? Certainly not.'

Angel looked completely unmoved. After all, in his job he had been lied to and sworn at by experts. 'And the young lady?' he said.

The bemused young woman looked from one man to the other and back and said, 'No. I'm sorry. I didn't see anyone.'

Angel nodded and continued the round. He eventually reached his wife, who saw him and looked concerned.

'What's happened, Michael? Is everything all right?'

'They want me to find Lady Muick's necklace. Are you enjoying yourself?'

She shrugged and said, 'Well . . .'

'I'm sorry, darling,' he said, 'but they've set me on. I can hardly decline.'

'I met Mr and Mrs Stewart Twelvetrees . . . well, Lydia came and sought me out . . . and Nadine. They seem very nice.'

'Good,' he said. 'I must get on. I'll come back soon. Try and enjoy yourself, sweetheart. Sorry about this. Offer to help Mrs Mackenzie, if you want to.'

She stood up and looked round. 'Where is she?'

'I dunno. Ask a member of the staff.'

Angel turned away and continued the questioning. 'Excuse me, have either of you seen anything of Lady Muick's necklace?'

He eventually came across Stewart and Lydia Twelvetrees with Nadine and he said, 'Oh, hello there. Can I ask if any of you have seen anything of Lady Muick's necklace?'

'No, Mr Angel, sorry,' Stewart Twelvetrees said.

'Delighted to meet your lovely wife,' Lydia Twelvetrees said.

'Yes, it was,' Nadine Tinker said. 'She is lovely.'

'She said she was pleased you had made yourselves known to her,' Angel said. 'We don't get out to meet people much, you know. Excuse me, must move on. I thought I was having an evening off. Instead they've got me working.'

Stewart gave him a friendly wave as he turned away, and heard him say, 'Excuse me, can I ask if any of you have seen anything of Lady Muick's necklace?'

He carried on with the same question all the way round the Great Hall, including the MC and the orchestra, with no success. It took him more than an hour and he knew he must have missed people coming and going to the dining room, the bar, the bathroom, or on the dance floor but that could hardly have been avoided.

He went round to Lady Muick's sitting room and tapped on the door.

'Come in,' the commanding voice of Mrs Mackenzie could be heard.

There was nobody there but her. She was at a table counting money. There was a biscuit tin filled with notes and coins, and several bags of coins ready to pay into the bank.

He told her what he had done and had to report that he had had no success. He then asked her if she had had any success with the staff.

'None at all. Nobody saw anything. Nobody knew anything. Most exasperating.'

Angel nodded. But it was no surprise to either of them.

'How is Lady Muick after all this?' he said.

'She'll get over it. But it's not a very nice thank you for her letting the townspeople of Bromersley climb all over her furniture and look around her home for free.'

Angel shrugged slightly and nodded in agreement.

'Well, thank you for your efforts, Inspector,' she said. 'But I am certain that we could have recovered the necklace if we had closed and barred the castle doors and strip-searched everybody, like I wanted you to do in the first place.'

Angel's face muscles tightened. 'It was not possible,' he said, 'we didn't have enough officers on hand to implement it, and by the time we could have made the castle watertight, the necklace could have been well away from the place.'

'That's not necessarily true, Inspector. The thief might very well still be in the castle.'

'He or she *might* still be in the castle. But, in any case, we haven't enough officers to carry out strip searches. It's the sort of thing carried out under certain circumstances in prisons. It's a huge undertaking, ordering perfectly innocent people — many of them elderly — to take off their clothes in front of officers, and then the officers actually examining them.'

'If people were honest, such searches would not be necessary.'

His eyes flashed. 'I know that. You tell *them*. Ninety-nine per cent are honest. It isn't reasonable to put the ninety-nine through the indignity of a strip-search. These people have paid money to come here to enjoy themselves. It wouldn't be reasonable to put them through such an ordeal. This is not yet a police state! In any case, it is not possible to do it. We haven't the authority and even if we had, we haven't enough officers of both genders to enforce it, so forget it.'

Her face was scarlet; her eyes were popping out of their sockets. 'You have been very vocal telling me what you can't do,' she said. 'Can you be just as vocal telling me what you *can* do?'

'There is still the opportunity that as people leave, they might get cold feet and discard the necklace. They might even report something they've seen or heard to an officer. We will have to see. That reminds me. The necklace could have been dropped into a lavatory cistern for later collection. I will immediately have them checked. Excuse me.'

He dashed off.

Meanwhile, the sextet played the last waltz, and many people left the Great Hall and made their way to the cloakroom. Stewart and Lydia Twelvetrees and Nadine were in the forefront of the crowd. They collected their coats and filed past the two burly policemen in their Day-Glo yellow jackets at the front door.

'Good night, officer,' Lydia said.

'Good night, madam,' the young policeman said with a smile. 'Drive safely.'

Stewart Twelvetrees went for the car while Lydia and Nadine stood near the main door hugging their wraps and purses, with several others. He soon arrived.

Nadine said, 'Come with me in the back, sis.'

'All right,' Lydia said. 'You don't mind, darling?'

'No,' Stewart Twelvetrees said. 'Be there in two minutes anyway. Are you in? Seat belts on?'

'Yes, drive on, Jeeves.'

Stewart Twelvetrees grinned and said, 'Yes, my lady.'

They went over the artificial moat and were on the long drive, but there were many cars ahead of them.

'Did you enjoy it, Nadine?' Stewart said.

'It was fabulous, thank you. It was nice to see all the dresses.'

'You looked very nice.'

Nadine smiled.

Stewart Twelvetrees said, 'Didn't you think so, darling?'

Lydia didn't reply. She was looking out of the window; her mind was elsewhere.

Nadine nudged her.

'What's the matter?' Lydia said.

'Stewart was asking you if you thought I looked nice.'

She frowned, then seemed to catch up with the thread of the conversation. 'Oh yes, sis, of course, you look terrific.'

Nadine wasn't sure that she really meant it. She pulled a face and shrugged.

'I did, really,' Lydia said to her. 'Pink always suits you.'

Nadine wrinkled her nose. 'It's blush pink,' she said. 'It's not just *pink*.'

Lydia's lips tightened. 'It's red, if the truth be told,' she said in a low voice.

Nadine's eyes flashed. 'It is not red. If it had been red, I wouldn't have worn it. You know what Mam said about girls who wear red!'

Stewart Twelvetrees heard the conversation and quickly said, 'We're nearly there, girls. And you both look like princesses.'

Nadine said, 'If I had had my own way, I would have had that green dress. I love anything green. Green is my favourite colour.'

The rest of the journey was made in silence.

Three minutes later, the car stopped outside their house.

'All change,' Stewart Twelvetrees said with a grin. As the sisters got out of the car he added, 'I think I'm ready for bed.'

'I've got my key,' Lydia said.

When the car doors were closed, he drove the car into the garage.

In the hall, Nadine said, 'I'm going straight up.'

Lydia said, 'Don't you want a drink or anything, sis?'

'No,' Nadine said. 'I must get to bed. I'm on early turn in the morning. Let's stop the fighting.'

'Yes,' Lydia said.

They exchanged kisses on the cheek.

'Say goodnight to Stewart for me,' Nadine said and then she went upstairs.

Lydia kicked off her shoes, went into the kitchen in her stockinged feet and put the kettle on. Then she came back into the hall as Stewart Twelvetrees came in from the garage and began to lock the front door.

She took off the plain chiffon stole and began to hang it over the newel post to take upstairs later, when something fell onto the carpet.

Both Stewart and Lydia saw it glint as it caught the light, and they saw it land on the carpet.

It was the missing emerald and diamond necklace.

Twelvetrees bent down and picked it up. 'Where on earth did that come from?'

Lydia went scarlet, not only her face but also her chest and neck. 'I've no idea,' she said. 'Oh, Stewart,' she added breathlessly. 'Oh, Stewart, darling. Let me have it. I'd like to see it up close.'

He passed it to her.

She snatched it eagerly, looked at it, checked the fastening, dashed to the mirror in the hall stand, held the necklace across her chest and said, 'Isn't it beautiful, darling? Isn't it the most fabulous thing you have ever seen in your life?'

He frowned. He was licking his lips. He shook his head. 'But where did it come from? I mean, who—'

'You saw what happened. It fell out of my stole,' she said quickly, then she looked closely at the piece. 'Look at those emeralds, such a deep, clear, green. Twelve of them,' she said as her eyes grew bigger and shone almost as much as the jewels. 'And these diamonds are what they call old cut. Look how many there are. They must be a carat each. And there are two, three, four . . . times twelve is . . . oh my God, there must be 120 carats of diamond as well. Wow!'

Stewart Twelvetrees's jaw was set, the corners of his mouth turned downward. 'But, Lydia, *where* did it come from? It wouldn't just fall out of the sky.'

His lack of interest in the splendour of the necklace annoyed her.

'Somebody must have dropped it into a fold in my stole, that's all I can think of,' she snapped, then excitedly she said, 'But look at it closely, Stew, isn't it fabulous? Green suits me.

It always has. It suited my mum. Nadine could never wear anything other than pink, to give her a bit of colour. She is always pasty.'

'Why would anybody drop it into your stole? Your stole isn't a pocket. And who would want to do that anyway?'

'I don't know. Look how the emeralds shine, how clear they are . . .'

'I'd better report it.'

Lydia looked up at him and pouted. 'Oh. Oh no,' she said and she gently kissed him on the cheek. 'Not yet, darling.' She kissed him again and again. 'Not yet. I mean, nobody knows we've got it.'

Twelvetrees said, 'Well, we can't keep it. Obviously. You'll have to take it back.'

Lydia pressed herself very close against him, pushing the top of her leg between his thighs. She kissed him lightly many times on the nose between the words she whispered: 'Nobody knows it's here, sweetheart. At least let me keep it until morning. Her ladyship won't want to be disturbed at this time of the night.'

He put his arms all the way round her, pulled her even closer towards him. Their lips met and they held the kiss for a little while.

'Oh, darling,' he said.

'Oh, I *do* love you,' she said.

They kissed again.

Then they just held each other with their eyes closed for a few seconds. Then he pulled away and, holding her by the top of her arms and looking her in the eyes, said, 'All right, darling, but you'll have to take it back first thing in the morning.'

'No, no, no,' she said, pouting her lips like a difficult child. 'I can't do that. She might think . . . she might ask how I came by it. You'll have to do it, sweetheart.'

He thought about it a while then said, 'I wouldn't be able to explain why I didn't report it to the police, or ring Michael Angel. She would know or find out that I'm a solicitor and that Dad works for the CPS.'

She was looking in the mirror, moving first one way and then the other, enjoying the way the stones sparkled in the light.

There was a noise from the kitchen. She looked up. The hall was getting warmer and steamy.

'Oh, the kettle,' she said. 'I forgot about it. I put the kettle on for us.'

She rushed into the kitchen.

THREE

Church Street, Bromersley, South Yorkshire
10.00 p.m., Monday, 3 June 2013

Detective Inspector Michael Angel was quietly humming the *1812 Overture* as he skipped down the steps of Bromersley Police Station, swinging three box files tied together with string. He was intent on delivering them to the Criminal Prosecution Service, only twenty metres away, two doors down Church Street. He saw the polished brass sign, walked up the path, pushed open the outside door and walked up to the tiny reception desk. He was almost at the exciting noisy part, almost at the end, where the cannons are fired, when he stopped short. His jaw dropped and his eyebrows shot up. Curiously, there was nobody behind the desk. It had usually been manned by a very plump young woman with glasses, called Tina, but this morning it was deserted. She was nowhere to be seen. He looked around. It was like the Marie Celeste.

Then he heard the hubbub of a crowd of people talking and the occasional clink of a glass. It came from the first door on his right. It sounded extraordinarily jovial and highly improbable coming from offices of the CPS in the middle of a working day. He pursed his lips, then approached the door and knocked on it. The hubbub continued unabated, and there was no reply. He knocked again, much harder. It was still ignored. He opened the door, looked into the office and saw between twenty and thirty men and women, mostly holding champagne flutes, standing around in small groups in the middle of the room, talking and laughing. The desks and chairs had been pushed to the sides of the room and were piled up to make room.

As he was taking in the scene, Mr Marcus Twelvetrees, father of Stewart, pulled him in to the room by his lapel and said, 'Michael. Come in and join us.'

Twelvetrees turned to a young man who was passing with a tray full of glasses. He grabbed two off the tray, pushed one into Angel's hand and held the other up towards the ceiling light. 'Cheers,' he said, and took a sip.

Angel said, 'Cheers,' and copied him, then he said, 'What are we celebrating?'

'Oh? You won't have heard,' Twelvetrees said. 'Juliet Gregg has been offered a partnership in the Osbourne chambers. She is only twenty-eight, you know.'

Angel was impressed. 'Very good,' he said. It was all he could manage to think of to say. He knew it would have sounded rather weak.

Twelvetrees said, 'It's fantastic! She'll be fast-tracked to be a judge, if I'm not very much mistaken.'

'Yes. I must . . . wish her well,' he said.

Angel knew Juliet Gregg. She was a high-flying young barrister, who was a beautiful brunette with an hour-glass figure, who didn't seem to need any make-up. Lately, she had assisted Twelvetrees in the Crown Court, prosecuting in some of Angel's cases. He thought that she was a quiet, thoughtful woman who only came alive when she was in the body of a packed courtroom. He had great respect for her apparent success at such a young age.

The string on the three files was pulling at his fingers. It reminded him of what he was doing there.

'I've come round to bring you the case notes for the O'Riley murder,' he said, holding up the files held by the string.

Twelvetrees' face muscles tightened. 'Not just now, Michael,' he said. 'Not just now.'

Angel didn't reply.

'There's some food over there,' Twelvetrees said, pointing over the heads of the throng. 'Do help yourself.'

'Thank you,' Angel said, but he wasn't the slightest bit interested in food.

'Excuse me, Michael,' Twelvetrees said, then he turned away and was promptly absorbed into the homogenous gathering of heads, all simultaneously nodding, smiling and talking.

Angel wanted to leave the files he had brought with someone responsible, then get out of the building and back to his office as soon as he could. He eased his way around the chattering groups, looking for someone he knew. Then suddenly, unexpectedly, he came face to face with Juliet Gregg, the star of the show.

She smiled . . . that enigmatic look . . . the mystery of a beautiful woman. 'Inspector Angel,' she said gently.

Angel held out his hand. Her small, cool hand gripped his firmly and shook it heartily.

'Congratulations, Miss Gregg. I hear it's a great promotion. I will miss you.'

'Thank you, Inspector. Thank you very much. But I will not be leaving Bromersley for a good while yet. And my new chambers will only be in Leeds, half an hour away.'

They exchanged smiles.

A man behind Juliet Gregg was pulling at her left arm and muttering something out of Angel's earshot.

'Excuse me,' she said as she was dragged away into the crowd.

Angel continued weaving his way through the chattering throng. Then he saw her. The fat girl called Tina. She was on her own, leaning against a desk that had a white sheet cloth spread out on the top of it, and on that were several plates of sandwiches, meat pies and sausage rolls. There were also serviettes, champagne flutes and paper plates.

Tina was eating a sandwich. She looked at Angel and tried to smile. She chewed rapidly to empty her mouth, and tried smiling again.

'Hello, Tina,' he said. 'I'm glad I found you. Are you enjoying yourself?'

'Yes, thank you, Inspector. These sandwiches are nice. Smoked salmon. Mmm,' she said. 'Help yourself.'

Angel looked at the spread. There wasn't much choice, but what there was looked inviting.

'No, thank you,' he said. Then he lifted up the bundle of files and added, 'I'll tell you what, Tina. I've got these case notes for the O'Riley murder. Will you give them to Mr Twelvetrees when the party's over?'

' 'Course I will, Inspector Angel,' she said, transferring a sandwich to her left hand to take the bundle from him. 'Any message?' she said as she pulled open the big bottom drawer of the desk beneath the food and lowered them in.

'No. He's expecting them.'

'You got that rotten so-and-so that murdered Mrs O'Riley?'

'Yes. It's the son-in-law.'

Her chubby face brightened. 'You are wonderful . . . the way you make out a case from nothing, bring the murderer to court and get a guilty verdict . . . *every* time.'

Angel frowned. He wriggled uncomfortably. He wished people didn't talk about him like that.

'I read somewhere,' Tina said between bites, 'where it said that you are like a Canadian Mountie . . . that you always get your man.'

He winced. One of these days he was going to be given a case that was actually impossible to solve . . . that would shatter his record and he would look a real fool.

'Well, Tina, I hope my team will always get the man, but the odds are that one day we won't.'

'Nah,' she said, and took another bite.

He waved at her and said, 'I'll have to go. Goodbye.'

He weaved his way back through the chattering CPS workers, solicitors, court ushers and clerks, and returned to the station. He went in through the front door, waved at the PC in the reception office who pressed the button to release the catch on the security door. He pulled it open and made his way down the long corridor to his office.

PC Ahmed Ahaz was standing outside the door holding a scrappy piece of paper. He didn't look happy.

As Angel drew closer, Ahmed sighed and almost smiled. 'Ah, sir,' he said with relief.

Angel sensed the young man had a problem. 'What is it, Ahmed?'

'Oh, sir,' he said, 'do you know a Mrs Mackenzie?'

Angel looked heavenward. 'Yes, lad. Why? What's up?'

'She's rung up, sir. Insisted on speaking to you. Wouldn't leave a message. Said it was very important. And would you ring her back as soon as you come in. I've got her number here.'

He handed the piece of paper to him.

Angel could see she had made a lasting impression on him. 'Aye, all right, lad.'

'Will you do it right away?'

Angel smiled. 'Give me chance to get to my desk.'

Ahmed nodded and dashed off.

Angel wondered what the old martinet wanted.

He went into his office, picked up the phone and tapped out the number. The phone was promptly answered.

'Ah yes, Inspector Angel,' Mrs Mackenzie said, 'I have just had a call from Lady Muick this morning. She has received a packet sent by ordinary post that contained the missing necklace in perfect condition. So there is no need for you to take any further action in the matter.'

'Oh good,' Angel said. 'Was there any message or address in the package?'

'No. Nothing like that. It was a local postmark.'

'Thank you for letting me know, Mrs Mackenzie.'

'Goodbye,' she said and the line went dead.

Angel slowly replaced the phone. He was pleased that the necklace had shown up. He was even more pleased to get that dragon off his back.

The phone rang. He reached out for it. 'Angel,' he said.

'There you are,' the voice said hoarsely. He promptly recognized it. It was his superintendent, Horace Harker. He started coughing into Angel's earpiece. Between short bouts of coughing, he said, 'A triple nine for you. Man reported dead in a bedroom at the Feathers. Doesn't look very nice. I couldn't get hold of you, then your phone was engaged, so I have notified SOCO and the pathologist's office to get things moving. All right?'

'Right, sir.'

'Get to it.'

He cancelled the call and tapped in a number.

Ahmed soon answered. 'Yes, sir.'

Angel told him about the triple nine and then instructed him to find his two sergeants, Flora Carter and Trevor Crisp, and instruct them to come to the Feathers hotel, ASAP.

Room 201, the Feathers hotel, Bromersley, South Yorkshire
11.45 a.m., Monday, 3rd June 2013

Detective Inspector Michael Angel opened the hotel room door, and peered inside.

Four Scene of Crime Officers in sterile white paper overalls, caps and rubber boots were busily working away in the bedroom. One was dusting for fingerprints, another was taking photographs, a third was labelling plastic containers containing samples, and the fourth was looking at a clipboard and checking boxes to tick off.

DS Donald Taylor, section head of the SOCO team, heard the door open, looked up from the clipboard and crossed to greet the Inspector. 'Good morning, sir.'

'Is it clear in here, Don?' Angel said.

'Yes, sir.'

Angel came in and closed the door.

'We've finished the sweep and the vacuum,' Taylor said.

Angel spotted the near-naked body of the half-dressed man on the bed. He was wearing only a white shirt, vest and socks. Most of the buttons down the front of the shirt were undone. The blankets, sheets and pillows were in great disorder, and one pillow was on the floor. His coat, trousers, shoes and underpants were on a chair in a corner of the room.

Angel gestured towards the bed. 'Dr Mac been yet?'

'Oh yes, sir. He's examined the body . . . he's ready to have it moved to the mortuary.'

Angel glanced round the small bedroom and frowned. 'Where is he?'

'I'm here, Michael,' the white-haired Glaswegian said as he came in from the en-suite bathroom wiping his hands on a white napkin. 'I'll be with you in a couple of jiffies.'

Angel nodded to his old friend, then turned to Taylor and said, 'Right. What have you got, Don?'

Taylor turned a page back on the clipboard and said, 'Well, sir, as far as we have been able to determine, his name is Norman Robinson, aged about 28, lives at Flat 12, Kyle House, Montague Street, Govan, Glasgow. He has a credit card on him but no money. He also has what might be his flat key on him, but no car keys. His mobile phone was found on the floor at the far side of the bed. Reservation was made for him here yesterday for one night. He arrived at about 1800 hrs last night. He was found by the chambermaid at about 9.30 this morning. The hotel has CCTV covering the main entrance and the reception desk, which I have commandeered . . . and that's about it.'

Angel nodded. He looked down at the body. It had a good head of black, wavy hair. The face was contorted. The eyes were still open. He looked closely at the lips.

'Mac,' he said. 'Take a look at the lips.'

Mac came across and peered downward. 'What about the lips?'

Angel said, 'Is he wearing lipstick?'

'It might be a slight burning of the skin by the poison, Michael,' Mac said.

'No,' Angel said, 'it's lipstick.'

Taylor came across and took a look. He put a pencil torchlight onto the mouth of the body, looked at it carefully, shook his head and went thoughtfully back to his checklist.

Mac said, 'Give me a chance to look at it in the mortuary. I might be able to get something on a slide to look at.'

'It's lipstick,' Angel said.

Taylor said, 'There's no lipstick or make-up or anything suggesting that in his valise, sir.'

As Angel pulled back from the bed he saw a white chalk mark in the form of a circle on the carpet on the floor just under the bed. It surrounded something small and round. He leaned downwards.

'What's this?'

Taylor nodded. 'Don't know. We're hoping for a print from it, sir,' he said.

'Is it a button?' Angel said.

'Looks like it.'

'It hasn't any holes in it. It's a fruit gum, isn't it?'

Taylor blinked. 'A fruit gum, sir?'

'Yes, I think so. A red fruit gum.'

'Is that the poison, sir?'

'Ask Dr Mac.' He turned to look at the doctor.

Mac said, 'I won't know that until I have it in the lab. Might explain the apparent appearance of lipstick on the lips, though.'

'It's lipstick,' Angel said. 'Any sign of the bag or packet anywhere? In the waste paper, in his pocket?'

'No, sir.'

Angel rubbed his chin. 'Means it was brought in by the murderer, then.'

Mac came forward and said, 'Let me have it. I'll have it analysed.'

'Right, Mac,' Angel said. 'After it's been checked for prints.'

'Right, sir,' Taylor said.

'Anything else, Don?'

'That's it so far, sir.'

Angel rubbed his chin and turned to the doctor. 'What you got, Mac?'

The old doctor sighed, then said, 'Well, the man was poisoned, Michael.'

Angel's eyebrows shot up. Poisoning was pretty unusual these days.

'At first, it looked like strychnine,' Mac said, 'but it isn't. The inside of the mouth is inflamed, and the condition of the bed linen and his clothes suggest that he was in severe pain before coma took hold. I'll let you know more when I've done some tests.'

'Right, Mac,' Angel said. 'Can you give me the time of death?'

'Aye. It would be between eight o'clock and midnight last night.'

Angel nodded and rubbed his chin.

Mac said, 'All right to move him, Michael?'

'Soon as you like,' Angel said.

Then he turned to Taylor and said, 'Do you know if he ate or drank anything since he arrived?'

'Don't know, sir. No signs in here of a takeaway brought in or dirty pots from room service or anything like that.'

Angel nodded. 'Right. Where's this chambermaid?'

'The manager's office. She's waiting to see you, sir, with the manager . . . he wants a word, sir.'

'I'll go down to his office,' he said and made for the door.

Angel went down in the lift and made inquiries at the reception desk. He was shown through a side door to an office at the back.

'I am the duty manager, Inspector: Jack Blacklock. This is Monica Spalding. She's the chambermaid attending the first and second floors. She found the body and reported it to me, and I reported it to the police station.'

Angel said, 'Thank you. Now then Monica, were you on duty when the man in room 201, Norman Robinson, arrived yesterday?'

'I expect I was on duty, Inspector, but I didn't see him.'

'Oh?' Angel turned to Blacklock. 'Do you know what time he arrived?'

'He checked in at the desk at six o'clock,' he said.

Angel turned back to the chambermaid. 'Monica, did you see him or anybody else enter or leave room 201 after 6.00 p.m. last night or anytime this morning?'

'No. And the only time I saw him was the once, this morning when I found him . . . erm, like that.'

'Tell me what happened.'

'Well, I knocked on the door several times between eight-thirty and nine-thirty, and, of course, there was no reply.'

'What time did you come on duty?'

'Six o'clock this morning. As I was saying, I couldn't get any answer, so at about twenty to ten, after I knocked and called out a couple more times, I unlocked the door and went in. I saw him on the bed. I called out to him. He didn't reply, of course. I went further into the room, closer up to him. I thought at first he might be ill. Then, I knew something was wrong. It was his eyes. Those grey-blue eyes were still open, wide open, staring at me. It was awful. It shook me, I can tell you. I came straight back out, and when I got my breath back, I reported it to Mr Blacklock.'

Angel nodded. 'When you were in the room, Monica, did you touch anything?'

'No. I didn't touch *anything*. I just wanted to get out of there.'

'Who cleaned that room the day before?'

'I did. Why, was there something wrong with it?'

'Did you vacuum the carpet?'

'I always vacuum the carpet if the room has been occupied. And it *had* been occupied. All the rooms on my two floors had been occupied.'

'I'll tell you why I ask, Monica. Something was found on the carpet at the side of the bed. It was only small. Can I be sure that it wasn't there after you had cleaned the room yesterday?'

She frowned. 'Well, yes, but what was it exactly, Inspector?'

'We are not certain yet, but it's about the size of an acorn.'

'An acorn? No. Even if I missed it with the vac, I reckon I would have seen it.'

'Right,' Angel said, 'thank you very much, Monica.'

'Can I go now, Inspector? I've my mother's shopping to do.'

'Yes, thank you.'

She nodded at the duty manager and rushed off.

Angel turned to Blacklock. 'Were you on duty when the dead man, Norman Robinson, checked in yesterday?'

'Yes, Inspector, I was, but I didn't see Mr Robinson. I can find out who checked him in, though.'

Angel nodded. 'Right. I need to speak to everyone who spoke to him. Also I'd like to know how he made the reservation and when.'

Blacklock was on the phone for a minute or two, then he came across and said, 'The young lady who checked Mr Robinson in last night is coming round now. Muriel Derbyshire. She'll only be a minute. He made the reservation only the day before yesterday by phone. I don't know that I can find out who actually spoke to him.'

Angel said, 'I really need to know, Mr Blacklock.'

The young man frowned. 'Maybe I can identify the handwriting,' he said.

There was a knock at the door.

Blacklock crossed and opened it. A young woman stood there. 'Come in, Muriel,' he said. 'The inspector wants to have a word with you.' Then he called back to Angel, 'This is Muriel Derbyshire, the receptionist you wanted, Inspector. I'm just going to check that other matter out for you, Inspector. Won't be long.'

'Right,' Angel called.

The door closed.

Muriel came in and up to Angel.

Angel smiled at her.

Muriel's eyes shone like cat's eyes. 'I've seen you on the television, Inspector,' she said, 'and in the papers. You're that detective that always gets the criminal in the end, aren't you? Like the Mounties.'

Angel was thrown off his stride. 'Er, yes. Well I usually do. I have done up to now. Let's hope that—'

'My mother says you're better looking than Tom Cruise.'

Angel looked away, then looked back at her and said, 'Oh yes? That's very nice of her. Now, I understand, Muriel, that you were on reception yesterday afternoon when a man called Norman Robinson came up to the desk. Is that correct?'

'Yes, that's right, Inspector. Well, it wasn't really the afternoon, it was six o'clock.'

He frowned. 'How do you remember the time was six o'clock, Muriel?'

'Because six o'clock is the cut-off time. That's the time we review all the bedrooms in the hotel that are not occupied or not paid for in advance. It is to avoid having any empty rooms that night. We usually have late inquiries for rooms on the phone between six and seven and even much later. And I recall that we were about to regard room 201, Mr Robinson's room, as free and therefore available to be let. But then he rolled up just in time.'

'I see. Please tell me what happened.'

'Well, as I said, he came up to the counter and told me his name and said he had a reservation for one night. I checked everything, asked him to fill in and sign the register, which he did. I told him his room number and said it was on the second floor and handed him the key.'

Angel screwed up his face and said, 'Yes, Muriel, but was he clean and tidy, was he rude, familiar or pleasantly courteous, did he look prosperous, down at heel or happy-go-lucky?

Was he handsome, desirable or obnoxious? Did he smell of anything: mint, beer, or soap?'

'Oh dear,' Muriel said. 'Well, he didn't smell of anything as far as I can remember. He had black curly hair that was very nice . . . and clean fingernails. I always seem to look at people's fingernails. He was quietly spoken.'

'If he had asked you for a date, would you have been pleased and accepted?'

She smiled. 'If I had been ten years younger and I wasn't happily married, Inspector, I might have gone out with him. Yes.'

'Did he look well-to-do? After all it costs more than a hundred quid a night to stay here, doesn't it?'

'If you include dinner, it does. I wouldn't know if Mr Robinson was well-to-do or not. I am not good at judging things like that.' At that point she looked closely into Angel's eyes and said, 'You know, Inspector, you *do* ask some strange questions.'

'I'm only trying to get a picture of the man, Muriel. One last question. Was he chewing or sucking anything while he was booking in?'

Her eyes partly closed as she wondered about the question. 'Like chewing gum, do you mean?' she said.

'Yes,' he said, 'or a sweet of any kind.'

'No, he wasn't. I can't stand people whose jaw is constantly on the go as they talk to you, especially with chewing gum. Can you?'

The office door opened. Blacklock came in carrying a printed sheet of A4. He looked very thoughtful.

Angel looked at him.

'If you've finished with me, Inspector,' Muriel Derbyshire said, 'I ought to get back to the counter.'

Angel nodded. 'Yes, I think so. Thank you very much, Muriel.'

She smiled, stood up and made for the door.

Blacklock came up to Angel. 'I feel a fool, Inspector. I took Mr Robinson's booking over the phone myself,' he said after consulting the sheet of A4. 'It's written down here in my handwriting. And it was made on Saturday — the day before yesterday — at 10.25 a.m. I can hardly bring it to mind, it was so straightforward. I do remember him giving an address in Glasgow because — as he spoke with a Yorkshire accent — I wondered why a man in Scotland would speak with a local twang.'

Angel's eyebrows went up. That was interesting. Norman Robinson spoke with a Yorkshire accent — possibly a local man?

'Was there anything else unusual about his booking?'

'No. Nothing.'

Angel wrinkled his nose. He thanked Blacklock and came out of the hotel office.

FOUR

Angel came out of the office and went to the hotel lift. He pressed the button and was taken up to the second floor to room 201. Angel found Don Taylor and two other SOCO men by the bedside cabinet. He noticed that the body of Norman Robinson was no longer there, and that Dr Mac and his big black bag had also gone.

When Taylor saw Angel, he said, 'We've just discovered something I am sure will interest you, sir.'

Angel came across the room to them.

'Look at that, sir,' Taylor said.

Angel looked at where he was pointing.

Taylor said, 'We sprayed a fine alkali spray across the surface of this bedside cabinet and it threw up these three ring marks: two the same diameter and the third slightly larger.'

Angel's eyes opened wide. 'A bottle and two glasses?' he said.

'We think so, sir. And we think it would be wine because the marks indicate weak acid.'

'Great stuff,' Angel said. 'And we *may* be able to determine exactly what sort of wine it was.' He reached out for the room telephone and was soon connected to the duty manager.

'Jack Blacklock. How can I help you, Inspector?'

'Can you tell me if any bottles of wine or any drinks at all were sent up to room 201 after 6.00 p.m. yesterday?'

'Certainly, Inspector. I'll just have to look through the list of vouchers from the bar and room service . . . no, Inspector. Nothing was sent up to room 201 yesterday.'

Angel wrinkled his nose. 'Thank you,' he said. He replaced the phone and turned to Taylor. 'No. I thought not. Is there a glass in the bathroom?'

Taylor smiled. 'We've checked it. It does not make the mark either of these two tumblers made.'

Angel said, 'Oh? So whoever the murderer is, he brought a bottle of something, and two glasses, and after they had presumably had a drink or two or more, the bottle and the glasses were packed up and taken away from the scene.'

Taylor said, 'That's what it looks like.'

Angel squeezed the lobe of an ear between finger and thumb. 'Very unusual,' he said. 'Sensible, from the point of view of the murderer, but very unusual.'

Suddenly he turned to Taylor and said, 'Make sure you get good photographs of those marks, Don. And measure the diameters.' Then he added, 'On second thoughts, take the bedside cabinet. Those marks could prove to be vital.'

'Right, sir. Leave it with me. I'll make it right with the hotel. We can move it ourselves.'

Angel nodded and said, 'Protect that surface.'

'Will do. There's something else, sir,' Taylor said.

Angel turned back to him. 'Yes, Don?'

'There are red stains, like flecks, on the bottom sheet of the bed. And it isn't blood.'

'Show me.'

Taylor pulled back a blanket and indicated the bed sheet covered with a clear plastic sheet.

Angel stared at it. 'It isn't face powder, is it?'

'I thought it might be that, but it isn't. If it were face powder, sir, it would brush off completely. This tends to cling onto the linen, as it were, as if it had an oily content to it. We've managed to vacuum some particles of it. It'll take a day or two to determine what it is.'

Angel frowned. 'Right, Don. Come back to me on that ASAP. It might be critical.'

'Right, sir. That's all.'

Angel turned away.

There was a knock on the door, then it opened. Detective Sergeant Flora Carter peered gingerly round the door. When she saw Angel, she sighed and then smiled.

'Come in, Flora,' he said.

She came in and closed the door.

'I wasn't certain I had the right room, sir,' she said. 'Sorry I'm late. I must tell you, there are five or six reporters on the front door.'

'What do you mean? Are they inside or outside?'

'They are actually in reception drinking, sir. But their eyes are on the front door. Nobody gets in or out without them knowing about it.'

Angel shook his head. 'Right, Flora. Thank you. I'd rather dodge them. I'm not ready to talk to them yet. By the way, on your travels have you seen anything of Trevor Crisp? I've an urgent job I want him to do.'

'No, sir, but if I do, I'll tell him you're wanting him.'

Angel sighed. 'Ahmed should have told him more than an hour ago. Well, I expect he'll turn up. Anyway, I've also got an urgent job for you.'

She beamed and looked at him attentively.

'Yes. Don Taylor has got CCTV that covers the front door and the reception desk of this place for yesterday, the day of the murder. Get it from him. And I want you to go through it — frame by frame — and see if you know anybody. All right?'

'Right, sir,' she said.

'Right, crack on with it then,' he said as he reached out for the room phone. 'Hello . . . it's Detective Inspector Angel. Can I speak to Mr Blacklock? Yes. Hello there, Mr Blacklock. I understand that your reception area is being monitored by newspapermen . . . I wondered if you had a rear exit I could use . . . ? That's very kind of you. I'll meet you at the bottom of the stairs in a couple of minutes. Goodbye.'

He went out of the room into the corridor and looked it up and down. He was looking for CCTV and there was none. He walked along to the end of the short corridor to the long one and saw cameras in both directions. He turned around, retraced his steps along the short corridor, past room 201, and made for the lift. There were no cameras there either. The lift was stationary so he pressed the button to open the doors and peered inside. There was the tiniest of cameras high in the corner. He came out and descended the stairs, noting that there were no cameras there.

At the bottom, waiting for him, was Mr Blacklock.

'Thank you for meeting me,' Angel said. 'I hope I haven't kept you waiting.'

'Not at all, Inspector. Not at all.'

'I see it is possible, if someone used the stairs, to access rooms 201 to 204 without being picked up on the CCTV.'

'Yes. That's right. I hadn't thought about it, but that's because they are round the corner on the short corridor by the lift.'

Angel nodded.

Blacklock said, 'You want to leave by the back door, don't you?'

'Yes, I do. If you don't mind?'

'No trouble at all. Please follow me,' he said, opening a door to the right marked 'Staff Only'. It led into a short passage past the 'Larder', 'Refrigeration Unit' and 'Kitchen' to a big door.

'Is any of this area covered by CCTV?'

'No, Inspector. And this is the back door.' Blacklock reached out, turned the knob on the Yale lock and pulled the door open.

It certainly led outside. There was the waste skip, the waste bins, the beer and lager crates.

Angel turned to the manager and said, 'Well, thank you very much, Mr Blacklock. If I wanted to come back in through this door, how would I do it?'

'You'd either use a key or press the doorbell and somebody from the kitchen staff would answer it.'

'And would they let me in?'

'Only if you were staff and they knew you.'

Angel rubbed his chin.

Having avoided the newspapermen, Angel arrived at the police station at 2.45 p.m. He let himself in by swiping his ID card through the lock on the rear door. He moved swiftly past the cells and turned into the green corridor. He arrived at the CID office and peered in. Ahmed was there, working away at a computer.

'Ahmed,' he said.

The young man jumped to his feet. 'Yes, sir?'

'What are you doing, lad?'

'Updating files, sir.'

Angel reached into his pocket and pulled out a mobile phone. It was still covered with silvery grey aluminium dusting powder. He handed it to him. 'That belonged to the dead man, Norman Robinson. Will you check on all the calls made from it over the past month, and let me know ASAP?'

Ahmed smiled and said, 'Yes, sir.'

'What's funny, lad?' Angel said.

'That's a much more interesting job than updating files, sir,' he said and turned away.

'Just a minute, lad. There's something else.'

He turned back. 'Yes, sir?'

'I asked you to tell DS Crisp I wanted him at the Feathers.'

'I did, sir,' Ahmed said. 'That must have been nearly two hours ago.'

'Well, he hasn't turned up.'

'Sorry, sir. I do know he was taken up with something.'

Angel frowned. 'What do you mean, lad? Speak plainly.'

'I mean he was busy with something.'

Angel's eyes flashed. 'We're all busy with something,' he said. 'Or we should be. I wanted him at the Feathers. He must think this place is Alton Towers.'

'I can try him on his mobile again, sir.'

'Please do that,' he said. Then he stomped out of the CID office, crossing to his own office, which was the door almost opposite.

Angel had hardly time to sit down, switch on the desk light and pull the pile of papers on his desk towards him when there was a knock on the door.

'Come in,' Angel called.

Crisp swaggered in looking amazingly bright and cheerful.

Angel glared at him with a face like thunder.

'*There* you are, sir,' Crisp said. 'I've just been to the Feathers, I was told you wanted to see me there.'

Angel's lips tightened back against his teeth. 'I did. That was more than two hours ago! Where the hell have you been?'

Crisp blinked. 'Well, sir, I got a tip-off that Harry "the hatchet" Harrison had been seen in the Fisherman's Rest on Canal Road last night and was actually staying at the King George hotel, on Main Street, with a girl. So I was investigating that. I'd been down to—'

'Why didn't you report it to me?'

'Because I knew you were busy with the triple nine at the Feathers.'

'What's that got to do with it? I sent out a message for you to join me at the scene.'

'Well, I knew that Flora would be there with you, sir. And I was sure you'd agree that such a tip had to be followed up promptly.'

'It probably did need following up promptly, but that would have been a decision I would have had to make. We all want to see Harrison behind bars, but you know he is rarely seen. Anonymous tip-offs are particularly unreliable and usually come when it is too late to act on them. Anyway, where did the tip come from?'

'On the phone, sir. I don't know who. I couldn't trace his number back because he'd put a block on it.'

'Didn't you recognize the voice?'

'It was nobody I knew — or could recognize anyway.'

Angel looked at him slyly. 'Not one of your private cliques of snouts?'

Policemen were no longer permitted their personal and private informants. It was supposed to prevent dishonest officers defrauding the taxpayer. Cash handouts of that sort had to be declared, and a careful note of the snout's name, address, time, the information received and the amount of cash handed over was held in a book. Of course, this did not entirely work as it should, and there were plenty of ways an astute policeman could sidetrack the account.

Crisp said, 'That's against the rules, sir, and you know that like you, sir, I would *never* do anything that was against the rules.'

He looked straight into Crisp's eyes. There was a dig in there somewhere that made Angel think.

'Well, what did you find out, then?' he said.

'I wasn't able to confirm what the informant had said, and Harrison — if it *had* been him — and his girlfriend had booked out of the King George minutes before I got there.'

Angel frowned. 'What do you mean, "if it *had* been him"?'

'Yes, well, the witnesses were . . . uncertain, sir.'

'You can get some good pictures of him from Records at the NPC. You could have shown them to them.'

'I know, but as the man had now gone, I didn't think it was worth spending any more time on them. I'd spent more than an hour on this . . . and I knew you expected me . . . and, by this time, I had heard that this was definitely a murder case—'

'All right, lad, let's be practical. Do you think there's a possible lead to the whereabouts of Harrison if I left you to pursue it?'

Crisp curled his lips as he thought, then he shook his head and said, 'He's probably covered his tracks most carefully.'

Angel nodded. 'I would think that he probably has. In which case, let's get on with the case in hand. And don't go wandering off like that. If I tell you to be somewhere, in future, be there.'

'Yes, sir.'

'Right, lad. Have you ever been to Glasgow?'

FIVE

Angel was struggling to reduce the pile of letters, reports and other police service paperwork that was forever arriving on his desk. At that present moment, he was trying to read and grasp the relevance to crime detection of a booklet, one of many, that had recently arrived in the post. On the cover in red in bold print it said: 'To be circulated to all senior police officers.' That wasn't unusual. All sorts of mumbo-jumbo arrived on his desk with statements of that sort clearly marked on them. This particular one was entitled, 'Home Office study relating to the proposal of granting voting rights of prisoners at UK General Elections.'

The Town Hall clock struck 5.00 p.m. He heard it and gladly closed the booklet, tossed it into the wastepaper basket, stood up, reached out for his coat and left the office.

He arrived home a few minutes later.

When Angel let himself in through the back door, Mary was in the kitchen.

'Hello, darling,' she said. 'Had a good day?'

He gave her a kiss on the cheek.

'All right,' he said. 'Got a phone call from a friend of yours,' he said as he hung his coat up in the hall cupboard.

'Who was that?' she said as she peered into the oven.

'The exalted and almighty, Mrs Mackenzie,' he said as he came back into the kitchen.

Mary smiled. 'She's not exactly my friend. What did she have to say?'

'She rang up to say that Lady Muick's necklace had been safely returned,' he said as he opened the fridge and took out a can of German beer.

Her eyebrows went up. 'Oh, that *is* good news, isn't it? Who returned it? Had it been stolen, then?'

'It had been stolen all right,' he said as he opened the cupboard and took out a glass tumbler. 'I don't know who took it, but it was returned by post, anonymously.'

'Are you sure it had been stolen?'

He poured out the beer. 'It wouldn't have been returned like that if it had been genuinely found. The finder would have wanted the glory, and possibly a reward, from Lady Muick.'

She frowned as she stirred the thickener into the gravy. 'No. I see.' She stirred vigorously, then said, 'Will you set the table, love?'

Angel put down the glass. 'Yeah, what we having?'

'Shepherd's pie and cabbage. And fresh strawberries, the first this season. And ice cream.'

It sounded good. He nodded, opened the dresser drawer, took out four table mats and began sorting out the cutlery. 'Is there any post?' he said.

'Nothing important,' she said. 'Don't bother with that now, I'm just about to serve up.'

She opened the oven and peered inside. 'It's ready,' she said. She glanced round the table to check it. 'Better get the salt. You might need it.'

Angel rummaged round the cupboard, found it and put it on the table.

Mary then turned the gas rings and the oven off and said, 'Sit down now, love. I'm serving up.'

After the meal, while Mary cleared away and made the coffee, Angel went into the sitting room. He looked on the sideboard for the post. There was no sign of any envelopes or post of any kind. There was, however, a pot figure of an animal or creature of some kind, that took his eye. He had not seen it before. He picked it up, then turned it upside down to see if there were any maker's mark or labels that might indicate what it was or where it had come from. It had four legs and one head, and was a dirty yellowish-brown colour.

He could hear Mary banging pans around in the kitchen and slamming cupboard doors.

'What's this on the sideboard?' he called.

'What? Oh, that. Isn't it nice? It's a present from Libby Copley, next door. It's from Tanzania, I expect. It's a sort of thank you for looking after their house while they were away.'

He frowned, put it down and sat down in his favourite chair.

'All you did was feed their goldfish and take in a parcel from Damart,' he said.

'I know, but it's a very nice thought,' she said, arriving with two mugs of coffee. She put them on the library table next to him.

He picked his up and said, 'Thank you.' He took a sip and added, 'But what is it exactly?'

'I don't know. It's an animal.'

'What sort of an animal?'

'An animal. It's a four-legged animal. You're so used to asking questions, you've started being a policeman at home.'

'It's a simple enough question, Mary: what sort of an animal is it? Is it a dog, a cat, a horse, or what?'

'I have no idea. Looks a bit like a hippopotamus.'

'It's nothing like a hippopotamus. They are grey, not that sickly browny-greeny-yellowy colour. It looks more like a lump of clay the potter had left over that somehow got into the kiln.' He took a sip of the coffee. 'Where are you going to keep it?'

'It's probably very valuable . . . an antique from the Ming dynasty or something like that.'

'Oh, yes. I can just see that, Mrs Liberty Bodice Copley giving you a ten-million-pound antique ornament for feeding their goldfish, Ernie, for two weeks.'

Mary breathed out impatiently, then shook her head. 'Look in the *Radio Times* and see if there's anything on tonight, Michael,' she said.

'By the way, where's the post?' he said.

'Oh,' she said. She was hoping he had forgotten about that. She stood up, went into the kitchen and returned with a brown envelope, which she gave to him.

As soon as he saw it, his eyes flashed. 'It's from the gas people,' he said and he tore into the envelope.

'That's why you've been holding it back,' he said. 'I thought you were up to something.'

'I wanted you to enjoy your tea and not get all worked up,' she said.

He wasn't listening. He read the letter very quickly then looked up at her. 'It starts all sweetness and cosy-cosy. Listen: "Dear Mr Angel, our energy tariffs are changing." Why don't they say outright that their prices are going up? They are putting them up by five per cent. They put them up ten per cent only six months ago. But they say they'll still be cheaper than most of the other energy suppliers.'

'It'll be the same for everybody else, love.'

'But we're not everybody else, Mary.'

'There'll be others a lot worse off than us.'

'Aye, and there'll be those who are a lot better off than us as well.'

'Well look, is there anything we can do about it?'

'Yes. We'll have to use less gas.'

Mary shook her head.

They sat in silence for a few seconds, then Mary grabbed the *Radio Times* and said, 'Well, do you want to watch television or not?'

He wrinkled his nose, pushed the letter into its envelope and tossed it onto the library table. 'What's on?' he said as he reached out for the television remote and switched on the set.

Up came the picture of a pretty woman newsreader. '. . . And that's the international news,' she said. 'And now the latest in the UK . . . a 28-year-old man was found dead in a hotel in the market town of Bromersley. The man has been identified as Norman Robinson, a single man, who originally lived in the town and had been living in Glasgow. He was apparently visiting his home town for one night only. We understand that the cause of death is not yet known, but foul play is suspected. The police have their top homicide detective investigating the case.'

'That's you, darling,' Mary said with a smile.

The newsreader went on '. . . The cost of gas is set to rise another five per cent in the autumn.'

Angel's knuckles turned white. 'We know!' he yelled as he ran his hand through his hair.

Mary quickly said, 'There's a repeat of an episode of *Bad Girls*. Do you want to see that?'

His face brightened. 'Yeah.'

Mary smiled.

It was 8.28 a.m. the following morning, Tuesday the 4th of June. Angel was in his office at his desk when the phone rang. It was Dr Mac.

'Am I too early for ye, Michael?' the Scotsman said. 'I was burning the midnight oil and I'm therefore in a position to tell you a few facts about the deceased, Norman Robinson.'

'Fire away, Mac. I am all ears.'

'Aye, well the young man died from asphyxia, that's certain.'

Angel thought that that was odd. 'That's smothering, isn't it?' he said. 'Suffocation?'

'Well, yes. It could be. However, in this instance there are no marks round the mouth and nose. I would have expected to find bruising or pressure marks on the skin if that had been the case. A constriction in the throat would be another explanation.'

'You mean like choking on a chicken bone or something?'

'Yes, but there's no signs of that either. I have examined the larynx and the throat most carefully. They are in perfect condition. The inhalation of smoke is another possibility, but there were no signs of smoke at the scene. Also it is not inhalation of carbon monoxide from a gas leak or from a car exhaust.'

'Well, what is it, then?'

'Put simply, it is oxygen deficiency. But there are many possible reasons for it. I thought at first it was a consequence of poisoning . . . but there is absolutely no trace in the blood. There are all sorts of thoughts in my mind, Michael. It is possible, of course, that if the victim was weak or had been drinking substantial amounts of alcohol or been heavily drugged that he could simply have been murdered by "burking".'

'"Burking"?' Angel said. 'And what's that, Mac? Or have you just made it up?'

'Indeed I hav' na' made it up,' Mac said. 'That is the term often ascribed to a killing method that involves simultaneous smothering and compression of the torso. The term "burking" comes from the method William Burke and William Hare used to kill their victims during the West Port murders. They killed the usually intoxicated victims by sitting on their chests and suffocating them by putting a hand over their nose and mouth, while using the other hand to push the victim's jaw up. The corpses had no visible injuries, and so were suitable cadavers to be sold to medical schools for money.'

'Could that not be the case, Mac?'

'It might have been, Michael, but there is no alcohol in his bloodstream, nor signs of any drugs, nor was he physically weak, nor were there any signs of a fight. It mystifies me, Michael, I have to admit. You'll have to leave it with me. There are a few more tests I can make, and I will repeat the tests I have already made. I'll let you know as soon as I know myself.'

'Right, Mac, thank you very much.'

'I can't satisfy the question of his sexuality either, but I *can* tell you that his genitalia are perfectly normal, as are all his clothes, so there is no evidence to suppose that he might be a transsexual.'

'Good, but what about the red stuff on his lips?'

'Lipstick, very high-quality lipstick, as it happens,' Mac said, 'and I think it arrived there as a result of somebody kissing the victim once or even several times.'

'And do you think *that* somebody was male or female?'

'How could I know that, Michael? I expect, being the naive one that I am, I would say it was female, but I really don't know.'

'And the red, sweetie-looking thing . . . had that anything to do with the cause of death?'

'No. The red sweetie-looking thing is a red sweetie, commonly described as a fruit gum, and as innocent as the day is long. So it was left by somebody who sucks fruit gums. I'll get back to you.'

'Thanks, Mac.'

Angel replaced the phone and pursed his lips. It was very unusual for Mac to be confounded by a cause of death. But the other info was helpful. Now he would really like to hear how Ahmed was getting along tracing the calls on Norman Robinson's mobile, and how Crisp was progressing in Glasgow delving into the victim's background. He was about to pick up the phone to call Ahmed when it began to ring. He reached out for it.

'Angel.'

'It's Flora, sir. I'm in the lecture room, going through that CCTV. I think I've got something.'

Angel's heart began to race. 'I'll come down,' he said, slamming the phone into its cradle.

He arrived in the lecture room to find Flora seated halfway back in the room with a solitary table in front of her. She had plugged the CCTV playback through her laptop onto the big screen and the sound into the enhanced replay soundtrack speakers. She had also quite sensibly closed the blinds to provide maximum clarity to the pictures being shown.

'Got him on the screen now, lass?' he said as he untangled a chair from the stack at the side of the room, carried it across to where Flora was seated, set it down and sat along the side of her.

'That character *there*, sir,' she said. 'I remember his face but not his name.'

She had frozen the CCTV picture. It showed a man in his twenties coming through the Feathers doorway. It was a clear picture and he was looking upwards, which provided an excellent picture of him for ID purposes. In the corner was printed the date and time. It read: 02.06.13. 8.30 p.m.

Angel raised his eyebrows. 'Yes, I know him,' he said. 'He's served time for something.' He screwed up his face and rubbed his chin.

'Let it run a bit, Flora,' he said.

The picture on the big screen showed the man walk past the reception desk and out of shot.

'Stop it,' Angel said, 'and run it back to where he first comes into the picture, then let it run to when he walks out of it.'

'Right, sir. But that will only run for two or three seconds.'

'That's all right, lass. Do it a few times. It might just shake my memory.'

As he watched the screen, he said, 'I do remember this lad. He was with his father and one other. They were doing the "leftover tarmac" scam.'

Flora frowned. 'What's that one, sir?' she said.

'Well, the scammers usually pick on the elderly or infirm who have a drive that is maybe a bit tatty. The most presentable of the team knocks on the door of the poor soul and says something like: "I was just in the neighbourhood resurfacing a drive, madam, and we've some tarmac left . . . just enough to even off your drive and smarten it up. It would normally cost around a thousand pounds, but we could do it for only two hundred pounds. Would you like us to do your drive?" '

'And I suppose some people fall for it,' Flora said.

'Yes, but there's more. They make a dreadful job of it. They just throw some tarmac over the drive any old how, they don't bother to make it even or roll it; then the whole team of three or four heavies knock on the door for payment. Of course there are usually protests but the bullies flex their muscles and scare the old folk, who consequently pay them. Sometimes they try to increase the price if they see the customer has more money than the agreed amount. When they've got the cash they make a quick exit. The poor souls they've swindled are often too embarrassed to admit they were taken in, and, in any case, they don't have a clue who the men were or where they came from. It's a despicable crime to aim at the old or disabled.'

'How was this gang caught, then, sir?'

'I think an old couple happened to catch sight of their vehicle and note its registration number, and our further inquiries subsequently brought the case to court.'

'I hope you'll be able to find out who this is and pick him up, sir.'

'Well, Flora, I'll buzz off and try to find the records of this case, and have this lad brought in. Well done, lass. Keep looking for any other villains. Also note the time that this lad leaves the hotel.'

'Right, sir.'

SIX

Angel picked up the phone and tapped in a single digit. It rang out a regular bleep. It was soon answered. 'Control room, Sergeant Clifton.'

'Ah, Bernie, DI Angel. I want you to send a couple of lads to 4, Sebastopol Terrace. Pick up a Thomas Johnson, wanted to assist us in our inquiries.'

'Do you want him in your office, sir?'

'Better put him in an interview room.'

'Right, sir.'

Angel cancelled the call, then checked on the address list on his phone, found Crisp's mobile phone number and clicked on it.

'Good morning, sir,' Crisp said. 'I was just about to call you.'

'Well. Where are you, lad, and what have you found out?'

'I'm staying at the Blue Thistle Hotel, Clyde Street, Glasgow, sir. And I've got started. I went to Robinson's flat last night. It's a bit rough, and it turns out that he was living with his girlfriend. Well, she called herself his partner. Her name is Michelle Brown. I introduced myself and broke the news to her. She was naturally upset and shocked, and she told me that she thought he was two-timing her but she had no idea who with.'

'Did she know he had come to Bromersley?'

'Oh yes. He had told her that he owed a bookie £800, that he was putting the squeeze on him, but it was all right because somebody in Bromersley owed him some money and he was coming down to get it. And that he had expected to get back up here by Tuesday.'

'Did he tell her the name of the bookie he owed money to, or the one who owed him the money?'

'No, sir. She also told me that he owed money on his credit card and was behind with his rent on the flat.'

Angel wrinkled his nose. 'Oh. Hadn't they *any* money coming in? Was he working?'

'No, sir. He'd had a job on the railway but had left it after a couple of weeks. He said it was boring, it didn't pay enough and that he was better off on the dole. Michelle had a good job in a supermarket in Glasgow.'

'Were you able to find out anything at all about the person who Robinson said actually owed him the money he came down here to collect?'

'No, sir. Do you think if I found his last place of work on the railway and went there, I'd be able to find out — perhaps from a workmate — who it was in Bromersley that owed him that money?'

Angel blew out a foot of air. 'I don't know,' he said, rubbing his chin. 'On reflection, though, I don't think he's likely to tell a workmate he'd known only two weeks something about his finances that he hadn't also told this girl, Michelle.'

Crisp nodded. 'I suppose you're right, sir.'

'What about his parents and other members of his family . . . and friends?'

'Michelle said that he'd told her that he'd more or less split from his family in Cheshire in 2009, and that he hadn't any friends. She's been with him a year and she's not seen any correspondence to or from anybody. He said he was a loner, and that had proved to be true, except for this mystery woman Michelle had said was somewhere hovering around.'

Angel frowned. 'Is there any way we can find out about this other woman?' he said.

'I'll have another try, sir,' Crisp said. 'I'm seeing Michelle again today after she's finished work. She might be holding back.'

'Yes. Good. Do that. By the way, in Robinson's flat, did you see any fruit gums? And have you come across anybody connected with this case eating fruit gums?'

'No, sir.'

'Hmmm. Well, see if you can find out anything else. Michelle might know more than she has said. The slightest morsel of information might help us make sense of the case, lad. Phone you tomorrow. Goodbye.'

He ended the call and returned the phone to its holster.

For the next hour Angel had his head down, busily catching up with the reports and letters on his desk, and made a little progress in reducing the pile. He was filing some letters away when he heard a disturbance outside his office. There were a few bangs as if somebody had kicked or thumped a nearby door, and voices were raised.

'I tell you I haven't done nothing!' a raucous voice yelled out.

'Inspector Angel only wants to ask you some questions,' another voice said.

'Well, you're not getting me into any frigging cell.'

'We're only going to an interview room,' a third voice said.

Angel got up from his desk, opened his office door and looked out into the corridor.

A burly young man in rolled-up shirt sleeves, who Angel recognized as Thomas Johnson, was being held by his arms and led by patrolmen PC Donohue and PC Elders towards interview room number 1, which was along the corridor two doors away.

'What's going on?' Angel said.

'This is Thomas Johnson, sir,' Donohue said.

'I know you,' Johnson said. 'You're that frigging Angel. It was you who sent me down last time. I'm not going down again.'

Angel stared at him and said, 'All I want to do is ask you some questions, lad. Now, we can do this the easy way or the hard way, which do you want?'

It took a few seconds for him to decide to answer. 'I want to go home. I've done nothing wrong.'

Angel stared hard at him. 'Which way do you want?'

There was another delay, then Johnson muttered something incomprehensible.

'What was that, Thomas?' Angel said.

'The easy way,' he bawled.

'Right,' Angel said, then he turned to the two patrolmen and said, 'Thank you, lads. Let him go.'

They looked at Angel a second or two then slowly relaxed their grip on Johnson, who shook himself like a dog coming in out of the rain.

'Come with me,' Angel said, closing his office door and leading the way down the corridor to the interview room.

Minutes later, Angel was seated at the table with Johnson opposite him. Patrolmen Donohue and Elders waited outside.

'Now then,' Angel began, 'this is simply a preliminary interview. I am not even recording it. Just tell me the truth. That's all I want.'

Johnson shuffled on the chair, looked downwards and rubbed his fingers, first with one hand and then the other.

'Where were you on Sunday evening between half-past eight and nine-fifteen?' Angel said.

'I dunno, do I?' Johnson said, making a quick upward glance in Angel's direction.

Angel pursed his lips. 'Think about it, lad. It's only the day before yesterday. *Sunday evening*.'

'I must have been at home. I hadn't any money to go out. Oh yes, I had. I had a win on the dogs. I remember. I *did* go out. But I was on my own.'

'Where did you go?'

'I'm not sure. Sunday teatime, Kevin brought a bottle round. We celebrated my win. Had a frigging laugh. I remember.'

'Who is Kevin?'

'Friend of mine, lives next door. He had to go home . . . something to do with his mother . . . no, it was his girl. He'd promised to take her somewhere . . . '

Several seconds passed.

Angel said, 'Where were you on Sunday evening?'

'I'm trying to think, man. I'm trying to think. Don't crowd me.' He ran his hand through his hair.

Angel rubbed his chin slowly. 'Did you go on a pub crawl?'

He looked up at Angel and said, 'Yeah. That's what I did. But I was on my own. I like to go out when there's a few of us. Nobody wanted to come. Yeah, that's what I did, I think. I went out.'

'What time did you leave home?'

'Frigging hell, I don't know. I had a bacon buttie then I . . . it must have been seven or eight o'clock.'

'Where did you start? Do you usually have a sort of regular plan, or a route?'

'We start at the Feathers usually, but I was on my own. I might have done. What's all this about, anyway?'

'Maybe you *did* start at the Feathers? Who did you see there that you remember?'

'The Feathers? There's that toffee-nosed bitch behind the bar.'

'Tell me about her, Thomas.'

Johnson shrugged. 'She was just . . . stuck-up. You know.'

'Did you speak to her?'

'Only to get a pint, you know. She did it as if I was rubbish, you know.'

'How much did you have to drink there?'

'I dunno, do I?'

'Did you go upstairs?'

'Might have done.'

'What did you go upstairs for?'

'I didn't say I'd been upstairs. I said I *might* have done.'

'If you *had* been upstairs, what would you go upstairs for?'

'If I'd had a woman, or I had picked one up. I might have taken her upstairs.'

'And did you do that on Sunday night?'

'No. I don't remember anything like that,' he said with a snigger. 'I would have remembered that, I'm sure I would.'

'Right, so what did you do next?'

'I remember coming down the steps and going outside. It was still daylight. There was a taxi in the rank. He brought me home, and I went to bed.'

'And what time was that?'

'I dunno. I don't keep count of every minute of what I do. I was out to enjoy myself.'

'You know when you were upstairs in the Feathers,' Angel said, 'do you remember going into any of the bedrooms?'

Johnson frowned. 'No. I don't remember going upstairs,' he said.

'You said, "when I came down the steps I went outside." Perhaps you went up in the lift, but walked down, and you forgot?'

'I s'pose it's possible.'

'You know, Thomas, it would help if I knew what you went upstairs for. Was it to visit a man or a woman?'

Johnson shook his head. 'I don't know any women there.'

He stopped fidgeting with his hands. He reached in his pocket and pulled out a small white paper bag. He fumbled in the bag and took out a small sweet and put it in his mouth.

Angel's eyes lit up. 'What are those?'

Johnson stared at him. 'Does thar want one?'

Angel leaned forward putting out his hand. Johnson grudgingly held out the bag. Angel dipped into it and took out a fruit gum.

Angel didn't put it into his mouth, instead he looked at it in the palm of his hand then slowly said, 'You are going to be in need of a solicitor. Do you have one of your own or do you want me to appoint one?'

Johnson's eyes narrowed. 'You're kidding, aren't you? What would I be wanting a solicitor for?'

'Is Mr Bloomfield your usual one?'

Suddenly, Johnson's face grew red and his eyes stared angrily at him. 'Yes, but what are you putting me down for?' he bellowed.

'I'm going to have to keep you in custody to assist us with our inquiries.'

'Oh no,' Johnson bellowed. 'You're friggin' not!'

Then he stood up, clenched his fists and lunged out a mighty right blow at Angel's face, which missed him by a mile. Angel managed to grab his arm and, using the momentum Johnson had created, dragged him flying across the table and onto the floor where he landed gracelessly in the corner of the room.

The ruckus caused the door of the interview room to be opened. PC Donohue stuck his head in. 'Everything all right, sir?'

Angel pointed with his thumb at Johnson behind him, who was on his knees, getting to his feet, shaking his head, and squeezing and rubbing his right arm. 'Pick him up and cuff him, Sean.'

It was with some difficulty that PC Donohue, PC Elders and Angel managed to get Thomas Johnson into a cell and then process him. It was necessary for Johnson to put on police-issue denim and remove his own clothes for SOCO to examine them. Again this caused more uproar and resistance.

It was not as if being locked up in a cell was a new experience for Johnson. Although, unusually, he had managed to confound the court on a charge in 2011, nonetheless he had served three months in 2002 for obtaining money with menaces and assaulting a police officer; also six months in

2009 for two offences of obtaining money by deception and assaulting a police officer.

When the three officers had completed these initial measures, Angel instructed the duty jailer that Johnson was to be left alone for the time being to cool off, and to give him the opportunity of recognizing the plight he was in and to come to terms with it. Angel then thanked the two patrolmen and instructed them to report back to their team leader.

He still had Johnson's mobile phone in his hand, so on his way back to his office he called in at the CID room and went across to Ahmed's desk.

'Check that off, Ahmed, ASAP. It belongs to Thomas Johnson. I've just taken it from his pocket. He's in the cells.'

'Right, sir,' Ahmed said.

Angel then returned to his own office, where he phoned and instructed Don Taylor to send a team of SOCO to search Johnson's home, 22 Sebastopol Terrace, for the usual things: drugs, firearms, pornography, excesses of jewellery, gold, silver, cash and items reported stolen, and to report back to him ASAP.

As he replaced the phone, it began to ring. He reached out for it. It was DS Flora Carter.

'I am still going through that CCTV, sir, and I have just come across that man again . . . leaving the hotel.'

'Thomas Johnson, Flora?'

'Oh, you found him?' she said brightly.

'Great stuff, Flora. What time did he leave?'

'9.15, sir.'

'Hmm. He arrived at 8.30 and left at 9.15. That would have given him plenty of time. Tell me, Flora, was Johnson carrying anything, like a bag?'

'No, sir.' She frowned.

The fact that he wasn't carrying anything worried him.

'I'm wondering, Flora,' he said. 'How would he manage to dispose of the two glasses and the bottle? We know they were in Robinson's room at the time of the murder, and that they are not there now.'

'Can't think, sir. Not just like that.'

'Right, Flora. Carry on.'

He returned the phone to its cradle.

He couldn't get the matter of the disposing of the glasses and the bottle out of his mind. He leaned back in the swivel chair and looked up at the ceiling. He rubbed the lobe of his ear between finger and thumb. Then it came to him in a flash. Johnson could simply have emptied the glasses and the bottle down the sink, rinsed them out, taken them with him in the lift to the ground floor, and then on his way out he could have dumped them almost anywhere on the floor, windowsill or any convenient ledge, and the busy hotel or bar staff would have collected them, and put the glasses in the washer and the empty bottle in the waste or the returns without hardly thinking about it.

He didn't know what the glasses or the bottle looked like precisely, he only knew the marks they made standing on a surface. Therefore he couldn't see much point in trying to see if any of the items could be located in such a large and busy hotel like the Feathers where there must be thousands of drinking glasses and hundreds of wine bottles. So that was decided upon.

All he had to do now was find a motive. Thomas Johnson's criminal speciality was extracting money by deception with menaces and assault, so one would naturally expect his alcohol-sodden brain to use the same modus operandi in his dealings with Norman Robinson. Maybe he simply tried to terrorize the poor man into parting with whatever money he had? Angel expected it might all be uncovered in the course of his further investigations.

The phone rang.

He leaned forward in the chair and reached out for it. 'Angel?'

'This is PC Tomelty at reception, sir. Sorry to bother you, but we've got a small crowd of men . . . newspaper reporters . . . there's five of them. They've been asking for you and they're getting difficult and noisy. Will you see them, or shall I report it to the duty sergeant and—'

'I'll see them,' Angel said. 'And be nice to them, Tomelty. You don't want to give the station a bad name. Is the interview room up there empty?'

'Yes, sir.'

'Right. Tell them I'm coming straightaway and show them in there.'

'Right, sir,' Tomelty said.

Angel put down the phone.

He rushed up the corridor to the front security door. He looked through the glass and found the reception area empty. He pressed the button to release the door, went through it, closed it and walked past the reception window to the interview room door. He pushed the door open, and there were the pressmen. He recognized one or two of them.

As he went in, they all rushed up to him and said something.

'Good afternoon, gentlemen,' he said. 'What can I do for you?'

All five men continued shouting.

'*Please!*' Angel called, holding up both hands. 'One at a time,' he said.

Suddenly there was silence.

Then he looked at a man he knew from the local paper, the *Bromersley Chronicle*. 'Giles, what is it you want to know?'

'I think I speak for all of us, Michael. We know a man's body has been found in a bedroom at the Feathers hotel. We understand that he was murdered. Can you confirm that and tell us about it?'

'I can't tell you much because I don't know much as yet. Tell me, are you all newspapermen?'

Three of the four others rattled off their names and the national papers they represented. The fourth said that he was a freelance stringer for a TV network.

'Thank you,' Angel said. 'Yes, there was a dead man found at the Feathers, and we believe that he was murdered.'

He then went on to tell them only facts that were not in doubt, which weren't many. It took only several minutes. At the end, the men asked innumerable questions: many were too intrusive, hypothetical or were not possible to answer. Angel politely declined to answer them and told the questioner the reason. He was very pleased that they didn't ask and he didn't mention anything about the finding of a fruit gum.

The entire process took about fifteen minutes, and he returned to his office a little brighter than before.

Ahmed was standing by his door. His face showed that something was wrong. 'There you are, sir,' he said.

'What's the matter, lad?'

'The super wants you, sir,' Ahmed said. 'He's had the entire station running up and down looking for you. He said he wants you to go to his office ASAP.'

Angel shook his head. 'He didn't think to ring reception then, because that's where I was. What's it about?'

'Don't know, sir. Sounds very urgent.'

Angel pulled a face. 'Right,' he said.

Interviews with Superintendent Harker were never enjoyable experiences for him. He had to endure them from time to time because he was his boss and he was expected to accept disciplinary direction from his superior in the same way that he doled it out to the ranks below him.

He trudged up the green-painted corridor to Harker's office and tapped on the door. Then he took a deep breath and pushed it open.

'You wanted me, sir?'

'Come in. Sit down. Where the hell have you been?' Harker roared.

Angel stared at him. The man standing behind that desk was ugly. He'd always been ugly. He must have been born bald and skinny.

At that time, Angel looked at the superintendent strangely, as if he hadn't seen him before. In fact he saw him almost every working day, sometimes up to ten times a day. But that day was different. The head he could see sticking up through that ill-fitting striped shirt with the limp collar looked just like a skull with big ears and a chin.

'I've been trying to get hold of you for half an hour or more,' Harker said. 'Nobody seemed to know where you were. Don't you ever tell anybody where you are?'

'I was in the reception interview room with five reporters for about fifteen minutes, sir. The lad on reception knew I was there.'

'Five reporters? I might have known you were wasting time somewhere having your ego massaged.'

He ignored the insult. 'I wanted the news of the murder of Norman Robinson to be widely circulated. And now I am assured that it will be all over tomorrow's national papers.'

'What on earth does that matter?'

'It matters a lot, sir. We have a suspect, but we haven't a motive. There's a story out there that we know very little about. It needs the players to show their hands . . . to assist us to fill in the blanks. I believe they will come forward. Anyway, the trap is now set.'

'Supposing you get no response?'

'I believe we will. If we don't, then we may not be able to solve the murder.'

'You think you're really smart, don't you? You never utilize the system created by the Home Office, HOLMES 2, specifically created for murder and serious crimes, which is extremely thorough.'

'It is extremely thorough, but it would be extremely costly to mount. For one thing, the system requires absolutely all persons associated with the victim to be put through the hoop. That's an immense undertaking. We'd need three times the men we have, for a start. More cells. More interview rooms. Bigger forensic department. So far we've managed to detect and bring to justice all our murder and serious cases without incurring that mountain of work.'

Harker knew that was true, and he really didn't want Angel to instigate the HOLMES 2 investigative programme. There wouldn't be any more government funding forthcoming, resulting in other services in the station being seriously curtailed. He liked to introduce the subject when the opportunity presented itself, so that he could enjoy battering Angel round the head with it.

'You are always singing that song, Angel, but you know that one day it could become compulsory. Then what would you do?'

Angel tightened his lips against his teeth. 'If you want me to introduce it, sir, I will.'

Harker's face coloured up. His bluff had been called. 'It may come to that in due course,' he said. Then he stuck a white plastic inhaler up a nostril, sniffled noisily, pulled it out, pushed it into the holder and put it in his pocket. He sniffled again, then expanded his face in a sort of smirk — he never smiled — to signify satisfaction with the process.

Angel stared at him.

Harker said: 'What I wanted to see you about specifically is that I see we now have a cell occupied at enormous public expense by a Thomas Johnson. Now, I don't want criminals enjoying a five-star lifestyle paid out of this station's budget. This isn't the Dorchester. I want him moving on, either despatched to the crown court, given bail, or sent to prison on remand. Has he been before the magistrates yet?'

'No, sir, but I can have him charged with resisting arrest, assaulting a police officer and damaging police property.'

'That would be a start. That's a fine, or three or four months tops. Well get on with it. What are you messing about at?'

'Well, sir, I am concerned. They might fine him, entrust him to probation and release him. In which case he'll probably abscond and I might never see him again. I'm hoping to get him for much more than that.'

'But you haven't the evidence?'

Angel shook his head. 'Not yet, sir.'

'That simply will not do. Do you realize that every day that lump occupies that cell, it costs this station £120? And that doesn't include legal representation, which for some crackpot reason is charged to us. I want him up before the magistrates in the morning.'

Angel's jaw dropped. 'I am most unlikely to get the evidence I need by tomorrow, which means Johnson might be released. That would be simply nonsensical.'

Harker glared at Angel. 'It would be nonsensical to keep him here being fed and accommodated a damned sight better than he would be at home, all paid for by taxpayers.'

Angel looked at his feet for inspiration. Then suddenly he looked up and said, 'If Johnson was released, and I am subsequently able to get evidence that he was responsible for the murder of Norman Robinson, think of what the newspapers might say: "Senior Cop ordered release of bully-boy murderer." I can see that in large print on every front page in the country.'

Harker's face changed. His eyes showed that he was clearly alarmed. He rubbed his chin roughly and said, 'I'll have to take that risk. Put him up before the magistrates and see what happens. I want Thomas Johnson out of this station by tomorrow afternoon. Have you got that?'

Angel's lips tightened back against his teeth. 'Oh yes. I've got it.'

SEVEN

Angel was pleased when the church clock chimed five. He had had a tiring day. His phone had never seemed to have stopped ringing. Also he had interviewed and wrestled with Thomas Johnson, been cross-questioned and pressured by Superintendent Harker, and apart from the discovery that Johnson was in possession of fruit gums and that that possibly linked him to the room where the murdered body of Norman Robinson was found, no new hard evidence had been uncovered.

He reached home by 5.10 p.m. and found Mary at the kitchen sink with the pot animal, the present from the neighbour next door.

He noticed that she was wrinkling up her nose as she looked at it.

'What you doing, love?' he said. 'Is it chipped or something?'

'No,' she said. 'I've just washed it and I was still wondering what it is.'

He shrugged. 'I ran out of suggestions when I first saw it.' He reached over her head to the wall cupboard for a glass tumbler. 'Why don't you ask Libby? She gave it to you, she should know.'

'I don't like to. She'd think it awfully ignorant of us.'

She wiped the pot animal with a tea cloth and put it on the draining board. Then she said, 'What's a wildebeest look like?'

'A bit like a buffalo, I think,' Angel said, glancing at the strange, ugly thing. 'That's nothing like a wildebeest. Any tea going, sweetheart?'

'It's in the oven. Be ready in about half an hour.'

He nodded appreciatively, then he opened the fridge door and took out a can of German beer.

'Any post?' he said.

'No, love. There was nothing. Do you know, I don't know where to put this. I've tried it on the sideboard, the mantelpiece, on the windowsill in the hall . . . I just don't know what to do with it.'

Angel looked at her. 'I know what you mean,' he said sipping the beer. 'It's not quite big enough for a doorstop. I suppose it would make a paperweight.'

Mary's face brightened. She looked beautiful when she smiled. 'A paperweight?' she said. 'What a terrific idea.' She pushed it into his hands and said, 'There you are, sweetheart,' and gave him a big kiss. 'It'll be useful in your office, won't it?'

Angel looked at it and frowned. It was ugly. He really didn't want it in the office, or anywhere else for that matter. He put it down on the kitchen table.

'Don't put that paperweight there, Michael,' she said. 'We'll be having tea in a few minutes. Will you set the table? Put it back in that box it came in. It'll go safely in your briefcase, then you won't forget to take it in the morning.'

He wrinkled his nose.

The following morning was Wednesday 5th June 2013. Angel arrived at his office at 8.28 a.m. as usual. He took off his coat, then opened the briefcase and took out the file of papers about the Norman Robinson murder he had intended looking through the previous evening but hadn't, although the case had been constantly on his mind. Then he saw the pot animal there in the box at the bottom of the case. He looked at it and his face creased. It really was ugly and totally indescribable. He lifted it out. From the pile of letters and reports on his desk, he took out a few papers and placed the monster on them. He stood back, looked at it, pursed his lips and shook his head. He turned the ornament round so that he was facing its backside. He looked at it again. He gave a little shrug, then he looked at his watch, picked up the phone and tapped in a number. It was to DS Crisp in Glasgow.

'Were you able to get any more information out of Michelle Brown about Robinson's other woman?' he said.

'Oh yes, sir,' Crisp said. 'She said that he had said that she was pretty well off.'

'Anything else?'

'That she thought she must live in or near Bromersley.'

'Any idea of her age?'

'No, sir. Michelle said that he'd implied that her parents and friends were loaded. So I thought they might be in business.'

'What sort of business?'

'I don't know, sir. I was only making a guess.'

There was a pause.

Angel said, 'Do you think you can rely on this Michelle, Trevor? Do you think she's telling you the truth?'

'Oh yes, sir. Of course she's got mixed feelings about Robinson now that everything has come out. He may not have been telling *her* the truth.'

Angel's mobile phone began to ring.

'All right, lad,' he said hurriedly. 'There's nothing more up there to be done. Catch the next train back. I'll see you tomorrow morning.'

Angel ended the call, returned the phone to its cradle and opened his mobile. 'Angel,' he said.

A quiet, smooth-as-silk Irish voice said, 'It's your old friend here, Inspector Angel. Is it all right to talk? Are you on your own, by yourself?'

Angel knew exactly who it was. He had known him years. It was Shifty Helpman, an elderly snout who popped up now and again with titbits of information, some of them useless and some of them extremely helpful.

'Yes, Shifty. I'm in my office on my own.'

'Well now, I've got fifty pounds' worth for you. Oh, you will thank me for it, Inspector Angel, like it came straight down from heaven, I promise you.'

Angel couldn't help but smile. 'Now, you know I would never be permitted to pay fifty pounds out of police funds, Shifty. I've said this to you many times before. Twenty pounds would be my absolute top and I must be permitted to value the item and pay you accordingly.'

'Ah, but this is really special, Inspector. I believe you're looking into the demise of a Mr Robinson, aren't you?'

'I can't mention names, Shifty.'

'I happen to know something about him that is important to your endeavours, Inspector, something that you will not know already and, I promise you by my mother's sacred grave, will almost certainly assist you to solve the mystery.'

'I confess you have my interest, Shifty.'

'Ah! Well, can you meet me in the usual place in, say, ten minutes?'

Angel looked up at the clock and then he said, 'Yes. I'll be there.'

Angel went up the corridor to the security door and let himself into reception. He went out through the main door of the station. The sun was shining and there was hardly a cloud in the sky. He stood on the top step taking in the view, and smiled appreciatively. It promised to be another dry, warm day. He ran down the stone steps to the pavement, across the road, down the narrow track at the side of St Peter's church, to a small gate. He pushed it open and it squealed a high note, and he noticed it squealed a lower note when it was closing. He took the flagstone path towards the vestry door, and then turned left to take him down the long area behind the church consisting of gravestones and bushes. It was very quiet there, just the rustle of the leaves and the occasional chirp of a blackbird or two. He walked quickly to the middle of the graveyard among rows of gravestones and looked around. Shifty Helpman was nowhere to be seen. Angel looked at his watch. There couldn't be any misunderstanding. He'd met Helpman there at least a dozen times before, usually late in the afternoon or in the evening when it was dark.

While he waited, he began to read the names on the gravestones and the dates of their deaths.

He was suddenly surprised by the unmistakable Irish voice of Shifty Helpman behind him. 'There you are, Inspector. You're by yourself now, aren't you?'

Angel turned to see the Irishman, who had appeared apparently from nowhere.

Angel smiled and said, 'I am indeed, Shifty. Now, what have you got for me?'

Helpman came up very close to him, so close that Angel could detect the smell of Algerian brandy on his breath.

'I knows what a great detective you are, Inspector Angel,' he said. 'Nevertheless, I think this will be very useful to you and well worth fifty notes.'

Angel looked into his bloodshot eyes and said, 'We'll see, Shifty, we'll see.'

'Ah, yes. Well now, you know that I get around and mix with all kinds of people. Well, the other day I was in company with Mickey "the loop" Zeiss, who is a runner for Harry "the hatchet" Harrison and does jobs for him. And I overheard the big man say that your Norman Robinson owed him — that is, Harry — very big money.'

Angel nodded. 'How much is that?' he said.

'Ten grand was the figure mentioned, don't you know.'

Angel blinked. 'Ten thousand pounds?'

'That's what I heard, Inspector. What do you think about that?'

Angel frowned and said, 'How did he come to owe him all that?'

'Mickey didn't say, but my guess is . . . it would be the gee-gees.'

'Is Harry a bookie then, Shifty?'

'No, Inspector. He buys debts, I believe, for very cheap money and squeezes the poor debtor dry for repayment of the capital plus a very high interest.'

Angel frowned. 'Does Harry do this himself?'

'You must be kiddin' me, Inspector. Harry don't do nothing. He gets Mickey and his heavy brigade to collect the dough.'

Angel rubbed his chin. 'And who is in his heavy brigade?'

'Mickey for one. I don't know of any others.'

'And who is Mickey "the loop" Zeiss?'

Helpman shook and his eyes shone as if he'd seen a ghost. 'I'd surely go to my maker if I told you, Inspector, and that's gospel.'

'Can't you tell me anything about him? I mean, what does he look like?'

'He's a short-arse little foreigner with a violent temper. That's all I know.'

Angel knew that was all the information he would be able to get out of the snout that morning. He put his hand into his wallet and took out a note. 'It's worth a tenner to me, Shifty.' He passed it over to the little man.

Helpman's face brightened. He showed no signs at all of disappointment. 'Thank you very much, Inspector,' he said as he gave it the once-over and then stuffed it into his pocket. 'I'll be in touch if I get anything else in your line. Goodbye.'

'Right, Shifty. Thank you. Goodbye.'

Helpman quickly made his way into the bushes and vanished out of sight as Angel came up the flagstone pathway.

As Angel arrived back at his office, his phone was ringing out. He dashed in and picked up the handset.

It was Dr Mac. 'Hello there, Michael.'

The doctor sounded unusually cheerful. 'I have some good news for you,' he said. 'I have at last determined the poison that murdered Norman Robinson.'

'He didn't die of asphyxia, then?' Angel said.

'He certainly did. He died of a severely deficient supply of oxygen to the body that arises from being unable to breathe normally. That's asphyxia. The problem was determining the cause. The blood sample showed no trace of anything untoward in the bloodstream, also there were no indications in the throat or the lungs. All this was greatly puzzling until I remembered. There is only one type of poison that produces such symptoms, and it is defined as aconite poisoning.'

'What's that? I've never heard of it.'

'It comes from a very common garden plant called monkshood which is a genus of over 250 species of Aconitum that belong to the buttercup Ranunculaceae family of plants.'

'Right, Mac,' Angel said. 'Thank you. You can pack it in with the big words. I believe you.'

He heard the doctor give a chuckle.

'Well, where did our murderer find this monkshood?' Angel said.

'It's a beautiful flower distinguished by its yellow monks-hood-shaped petals. The entire plant is poisonous . . . leaves, stalk, root, petals. And the poison can be ingested through the skin, causing symptoms that would require attention from a medical team, so great care would have had to be taken when handling it. There's some in my garden and probably yours.'

'There's none in my garden unless it's a weed. And how would my murderer have applied it, Mac?'

'It's not a weed. Well, he would simply squeeze the sap out of stems of the plant. For this he would have had to wear substantial rubber gloves. He would have transferred the gooey stuff to a container, typically a small glass bottle, then added it to something with a strong flavour such as cocoa, cough medicine, or some form of alcoholic drink. Death would have been very painful. That's why the victim's clothes and the bed were in such disarray. After a time, there would have been malfunctioning of the heart, followed by coma and then death.'

'How much time would elapse between him drinking the poison and being dead?'

'About an hour.'

'Did you find any food in his stomach?'

'No. He had not eaten for some time, maybe six hours. The poison may have been administered in alcohol, which would also to some extent tranquillize him.'

Angel nodded. It fitted in to some degree with the evidence already discovered from the marks on the top of the bedside cabinet.

'Well, thank you, Mac,' he said drily. 'All I have to do is find out those people who have monkshood in their garden.'

Mac smiled. 'That's all, Michael,' he said. 'Good luck.'

Angel ended the call. It had at last been established that the cause of the murder was poison and that the poison was monkshood. There was also a hint that the murderer could be a henchman of Harry 'the hatchet' Harrison, such as Mickey 'the loop' whoever he was, or Thomas Johnson, who was not known to have any connection with Harrison. Angel saw that if he could make a connection between the two, he could have a pretty good case. At this stage, he also had to consider whether it was likely that Johnson knew Norman Robinson and decide whether or not it was probable that they shared a bottle of wine or booze of some kind together.

He reached out for the phone. He rang Thomas Johnson's solicitor, Bloomfield, and made arrangements for him to come to the station as soon as possible so that Angel could interview his client. Bloomfield said he could be there in about half an hour. He ended the call.

Angel was adamant that he must attain clearer answers from the man.

There was a knock at the door. Angel glanced at it, then placed the pot monster in a more prominent position on his desk so that it could not fail to be seen.

'Come in,' he said.

It was Ahmed.

'Yes, Ahmed?' Angel said.

'Good morning, sir,' Ahmed said. He immediately spotted the pot animal.

Angel watched him.

There was a slight frown on Ahmed's face as he peered at it.

'Very nice, sir,' he said. 'Your new paperweight. Is it a sort of rhinoceros?'

Angel said, 'Is it?'

'No. Of course it isn't, sir. I wasn't thinking. It's an African animal, isn't it? Must be very rare.'

Angel shook his head. 'What did you want, lad?' he said.

'Oh, yes. I've just finished checking off all the calls made from Norman Robinson's mobile over the last thirty days, sir,' he said, waving two sheets of A4 with his close-written handwriting on them.

Angel's face brightened. The timing was perfect. 'Ah yes,' he said. 'Sit down,' he said indicating the chair. 'We can go through them now.'

Ahmed came in eagerly and took the seat opposite.

'He didn't make many calls compared with most people these days, sir,' Ahmed said, referring to his notes. 'And I don't think you would describe any of them as "social" calls to friends or just to chat. There were six calls to takeaways and shops or supermarkets. There were fifteen calls — of very short duration — to a bookie in Glasgow called Burns.'

'I expect they were always in the afternoon?'

Ahmed's eyebrows shot up. 'As a matter of fact, they were, sir. How could you possibly know that?'

'The fact the calls were short suggested that they were bets, placed just before a race started. Most racing is in the afternoon.'

'Oh yes, sir. Mmm, I see.'

Angel smiled. 'What else?'

'There are four calls to the Work and Pensions office in Glasgow.'

'I suppose they would be inquiries about work or dole money.'

'Then there were two very interesting calls he made, sir. One to the CPS in Bromersley, and—'

Angel blinked in surprise. 'In *Bromersley*?' he said. He quickly reached out for his pen. 'Give me the details.'

'It was Friday morning, sir, May 31st. The call was at 11.30 a.m. and lasted four minutes.'

Angel scribbled the details on a used envelope and put it back in his pocket. 'That's remarkable, Ahmed. You said there were *two* interesting calls; what was the other?'

'That was to the Feathers, sir, on Saturday morning, June 1st at 10.25 a.m.'

Angel nodded. 'Hmm. That would be to book a room for Sunday night. Anything else?'

'Yes, sir. There was a call to the inquiry line at Doncaster Racecourse. It's a recorded message that tells the caller the times and dates of forthcoming race meetings.'

'Hmm. Maybe he fancied a trip out there while he was back in Yorkshire?'

The phone rang. Angel looked at it and frowned.

Then he looked at Ahmed. 'Are there any more, lad?'

'No, sir,' he said, getting to his feet. 'That's the lot.'

'Thanks. That's a good job. Just a minute.' He picked up the phone and said, 'Angel.'

It was DS Taylor on the line.

'Hold on a minute, Don,' Angel said.

He turned back to Ahmed. 'Now, how long are you going to be with Johnson's mobile?'

'I should be able to do it by about three o'clock this afternoon, sir. It depends how many calls there are on it.'

'Aye. Right, lad. As soon as you can. Crack on with it.' He indicated with his thumb to Ahmed to leave.

'I'm off, sir,' Ahmed said.

Angel watched the young man glance curiously at the pot monster as he picked up his papers and his pen. He saw him peer at the other side of the ornament, then shake his head, and finally closed the door behind him.

Angel smiled into the phone, then said, 'What have you got, Don?'

Taylor said, 'Got a result from Wetherby lab on those samples retrieved from the bottom sheet on the victim's bed, sir. The palynologist there says that it's pollen from white oriental lilies.'

Angel's face creased. 'White oriental lilies?' he said, running his hand through his hair. 'White oriental lilies? Well, there weren't any flowers in the room, were there? Are you sure the hotel staff didn't remove them before you arrived at the scene?'

'The chambermaid assured me that everything had been left as it was found, sir. She was that upset and squeamish that I doubt she went back into the room after she had discovered the body.'

'Somebody else might have. I'll check on that, Don . . . pollen from white oriental lilies. I don't understand.'

'Pollen easily drops off the flowers, sir, and stains very readily.'

Angel wasn't pleased. That latest information created more confusion in his mind about trying to find the murderer. 'How did the pollen get there?' Angel said. 'Why was it there? Why was the source of the pollen removed?'

'Sorry, sir. I can't throw any more light on it.'

'All right, Don,' Angel said. 'Thank you.'

He replaced the phone, then sighed, then squeezed the lobe of his ear between finger and thumb.

A few moments later, he picked up the phone and tapped in a number. It was to the mortuary. He asked for Dr Mac.

'Hello there, Michael,' Mac said. 'I was about to ring you. That sample fruit gum taken from Thomas Johnson's coat pocket is an exact match with the one found by Robinson's bed. There are five flavours, or colours, and I analysed a cherry one because the one found was cherry flavoured, or red in colour.'

'That's great. Thanks, Mac. I note what you say.'

'I'll send it in my written report in due course. But I knew you'd want to know.'

'Yes, indeed. I'm interviewing Thomas Johnson later today. Of course I can't put too much weight on that because millions of fruit gums in all flavours and colours are made and sold every day.'

'I think that's true, Michael,' Mac said.

Angel then reported the finding of pollen on the victim Robinson's bed and asked Mac for his observations.

'It doesn't have any forensic connotations to any criminal activity that I can think of, Michael,' he said. 'I mean, neither the pollen nor the leaves of oriental lilies have been used as a poison that I know of. However, I am sure you will be aware that when pollen is found on a long-lost corpse, in conjunction with a pollen calendar the month or week or date of death can be approximated with accuracy. There's a whole department in some forensic laboratories dedicated to "forensic palynology", as it is called.'

'Yes, Mac, but . . . I mean, you can't murder anybody with a single or a bunch of white oriental lilies, can you?'

'I shouldn't think so. I have certainly never heard of it.'

'Well, is there any valid reason why a villain intent on murdering Robinson would come into his room with a bunch of flowers?'

'Canna think of any. Unless there was a bomb in the middle of them, and there's no evidence of that in this case, is there?'

'Quite. There's something else, Mac. Aren't white oriental lilies to be found at funerals?'

'Aye. I believe they are. I seem to remember my great-aunt Bridget's coffin was smothered in white lilies when I went to her funeral in Paisley thirty-odd years ago. Are you thinking that the murderer brought them as a warning signal to Robinson before he poisoned him?'

Angel bit his lower lip. 'I'm not at all sure; then again I'm not sure of anything. I mean, would a man bring another man flowers?'

'Not unless they were gay. And then I'm not sure he would. Anyway, Michael, in my examination of the corpse, I have discovered no forensic evidence to support that theory.'

'Hmm. I'm beginning to think that it might be a woman who brought the flowers.'

'It's more logical.'

'That means it's possible that a woman committed the murder. I know that that was always possible, but I always assumed the murderer was a man. Come to think of it, it is women who usually use poison, isn't it?'

'Aye. It is.'

'I'm seriously beginning to think that maybe I shouldn't be holding Thomas Johnson.'

'You're the boss, Michael.'

Angel pulled a face. 'Huh! And don't I know it,' he said. 'Thanks, Mac, anyway. 'Bye.'

He banged down the handset.

EIGHT

Angel picked up the phone and tapped in Ahmed's number in the CID room. 'Is DS Carter there?'

'I'll get her, sir . . . here she is.'

'Flora, I'm expecting Bloomfield in a few minutes so that I can interview Thomas Johnson, who is in a cell. Let them talk privately, of course, but when they are ready will you show them into interview room number 1 and then let me know? If Johnson is troublesome, get some help. And I'll want you to sit in with me to make up a foursome. All right?'

'Right, sir,' Flora Carter said.

Ten minutes later, the four were seated in interview room number 1.

The recording tape was running through the reel-to-reel, the red light was on, Angel rattled off the details of who was present, the time, date and place and then he began.

'Mr Johnson,' he said. 'The CCTV recording proves that you were in the Feathers hotel on the night and at the time that Norman Robinson was murdered. A sample fruit gum taken from contents of your coat pocket matches exactly with the one found on the floor in Robinson's room. What do you say to that?'

Johnson glared at Angel, screwed up his face and said, 'I can't explain it like that. All I know is that I didn't go anywhere in any bedroom in that hotel, that night or any other night.'

Bloomfield said, 'Also, Inspector, those fruit gums are extremely popular. They're made by a factory in east London where they make millions and distribute them not only in the UK but all over the world. Anybody could have dropped that fruit gum in the bedroom. It could even have been left by the previous occupant.'

'The chambermaid said that she was sure it wasn't left over from the previous day.'

'Well, Inspector,' Bloomfield said. 'That would be a bad reflection on her capability and thoroughness as a chambermaid if it had been, wouldn't it? One would have expected her to say that.'

'Nevertheless, Mr Bloomfield. The fact that your client was present in the hotel at that critical time, and the presence of the fruit gum at the murder scene and the fact that he had a pocketful of those identical fruit gums, is noted and cannot be ignored.' He looked at Johnson and said, 'Now, moving on . . . who paid you to murder Norman Robinson?'

'Nobody. I don't know nothing about it.'

'Was it Harry "the hatchet" Harrison?'

Johnson's jaw dropped open.

Angel saw fear in his eyes.

'No,' Johnson said. 'Never heard of him.'

'What did you do with the bottle and the two glasses?'

'Don't know what you're talking about.'

'What was the point of taking flowers to him?'

Johnson shrugged his shoulders, frowned and looked at Bloomfield.

'I don't know what he's on about.'

'You refuse to answer my questions?' Angel said. 'A search of your house, 4, Sebastopol Terrace, revealed a cache of money, £780 hidden in a biscuit tin, under a loose floorboard under your bed.'

Johnson leaped to his feet. His face was scarlet. 'You frigging bastards,' he said, all teeth and saliva. 'What right have you to go and search my house and take the only money I have in the world away from me?'

Bloomfield pulled at Johnson's jacket. 'Sit down, Mr Johnson. Come on. Sit down.'

Angel was unmoved. He stared at Johnson and said, 'Where did you get the money from?'

'I saved it up.'

'Do you work for Harry "the hatchet" Harrison? Are you one of his thugs? Is that money the money he paid you to murder Norman Robinson?'

'What the frigging hell are you talking about? No! Of course it isn't. It's my savings.'

Angel said, 'How did you save it?'

'I put a fiver or a tenner out of my money there every week.'

'But it's all in twenties,' Angel said. 'New twenties. In *consecutive* order. Withdrawn from the Northern Bank. Fresh from the mint. Only printed a month ago.'

Johnson looked at Angel and licked his lips.

Bloomfield whispered in his ear. He replied similarly.

The solicitor said, 'My client says that he recently took his savings to the Northern Bank and asked them to exchange them for clean twenty-pound notes.'

'Oh, really?' Angel said. 'Just a minute, Mr Bloomfield, did I say the Northern Bank?'

'You did.'

'What a fool I am. I'm so sorry. It wasn't the Northern Bank, it was the Westminster Bank.'

Flora Carter swallowed a smile.

Johnson leaped to his feet again. 'You rotten bastard, Angel,' he said. 'Trying to trick me, aren't you?'

Bloomfield grabbed his client by the sleeve. 'Leave it, Mr Johnson. It's not very important. I expect you forgot which bank it was,' he said. Then he added heavily, 'Just as Inspector Angel also forgot which bank it was.'

'Where did you get the money from, Mr Johnson?' Angel said.

'I've told you. I saved it up.'

'You're not a very good liar, are you, lad?' Angel said, rubbing his chin forcefully.

Johnson's eyes stood out like fried eggs in a pan.

'Don't answer that, Mr Johnson,' Bloomfield said. Then he looked at Angel and said, 'You know, Inspector, that's a very improper question. I must ask you to withdraw it.'

'Very well,' Angel said with a shrug.

He had no intention of withdrawing it.

'Interview ended at 13.22,' Angel said and he switched off the tape.

There was a knock on the office door.

Angel looked up from his chair. He looked as if he'd eaten a plate of fish pie from Strangeways cookhouse. 'Come in,' he called.

It was Flora Carter.

'He's back in his cell, sir. It took three of us to get him in.'

Angel shook his head.

'Where do we go from here, sir?' she said, casting an inquisitive look over his desk. She espied the monster holding down a few letters on the desk. Her eyebrows shot up. 'Ah, you have a new paperweight, sir.' She picked it up. 'Can I have a look?'

Angel nodded and leaned back in the chair. He had a lot on his mind.

'Oh, it's a mythological figure isn't it?'

'I don't know.'

'Is it that wolf that has snakes growing from its head instead of hair?'

'Don't know.'

'Something to do with Romulus and Remus?'

Angel blinked, leaned forward and looked at her. 'I don't think so. Do you like it?'

She hesitated. 'It's very attractive in a way. Quirky. Like modern art.'

He peered at her. 'Would you like it, Flora?'

She looked down at Angel, realized he was serious and quickly replaced the ornament onto his desk. 'Oh, no, sir. Thank you very much.'

He sniffed.

'I have nowhere to put it,' she added. 'It's very beautiful, though.'

He sighed, nodded, rubbed his chin and looked back at the ceiling. 'You know, Flora, I don't think Thomas Johnson murdered Robinson. I have to agree that the presence of the fruit gum in the room does not necessarily tie him to have been present in the room. It isn't as if we had his fingerprints on the sweet. However, he was present in the building. He doesn't deny that any more. And therefore may I be forgiven for suspecting that he was there for some nefarious purpose? I can't put my finger on it, but if he didn't murder Robinson he was there for some other criminal reason.'

'And somehow,' she said, 'I can't see him carrying a bunch of oriental lilies.'

He nodded.

'Are you going to let him go, sir?'

'I have still to find out what was on his mobile phone. If there is nothing helpful on there, I might have to. The murder was committed by somebody with intelligence, Flora, somebody who can organize themselves. Johnson couldn't organize a penny raffle. Nor could he save £780. I expect that that money had originally been a bigger sum such as £1,000 for doing something simple, like being a lookout man for a big cheese like Harry Harrison.'

'Well, where does Harrison fit into this crime, sir?'

'You know, Flora, I don't know. I didn't believe for one moment that Johnson had never heard of Harry Harrison. It is still possible that Johnson is regularly in his employ as a debt collector, bully-boy or minder. The only motive there is, as far as I can see, for him murdering Robinson is that he owed Harry "the hatchet" Harrison money and that he couldn't or wouldn't pay it back.'

'Well, what did he come back from Glasgow for, sir?'

'His girlfriend in Glasgow, Michelle, said that Robinson came to Bromersley to collect some money he was owed, but she didn't know who owed it to him. Anyway, it's a certainty he won't get it now. And I think we'll have to let Thomas Johnson walk, even though he's the only one we've caught sucking a fruit gum.'

'Do you want me to do the honours, sir?'

'Not yet, Flora. There are a few jobs I want you to do before we release him. I want you to attend to them yourself and to take this particular operation under your wing. All right?'

Flora Carter looked at Angel intently. She looked forward to the prospect of taking some responsibility in the case.

Angel said, 'Here's what I want you to do . . .'

Angel opened the big door of the CPS and made his way up to the receptionist, Tina, who looked bigger than ever.

She smiled at him, showing her two cute dimples.

'Hello, Inspector. Nice to see you. We're not expecting you, are we? You're not down in my book.'

At that moment, an office door opened and Marcus Twelvetrees came out, all dressed in white and carrying a tennis racquet and a valise.

'Ah, Tina,' he said. 'Any calls for me, transfer to Miss Gregg's office.'

'Right, Mr Twelvetrees,' she said.

He saw Angel and was surprised. 'Hello there, Inspector. Did you want me? I have to be off, else I'm going to be late. I'm meeting the Chief Constable about the . . . erm . . .'

'That's all right, Mr Twelvetrees, I came to see Tina, really. But as you're here, a quick question, if you don't mind? Does the name Norman Robinson ring any bells with you?'

Twelvetrees waved his racquet at him as he made for the door. 'Norman Robinson? No. I don't think so.'

'Has he been in touch with you by phone recently?'

'Me? By phone? Recently? No. No. He hasn't. Look, it's almost half-past. I'm sorry, Inspector, I'll have to go.'

'Thank you, Mr Twelvetrees. That's all right. Enjoy your . . . erm, erm . . .'

The front door banged and Marcus Twelvetrees LLD had gone.

Angel turned back to the reception desk. 'Now then, Tina. I'm making an inquiry about a case I'm dealing with. Last Friday morning at 11.30, a man called Norman Robinson spoke to somebody on the phone at this number. It lasted four minutes. All I want to know is, who did he speak to?'

Tina frowned. She drew in a long breath and breathed it out while her face showed that she had no idea. 'I don't know, Inspector. I get hundreds of calls a week on this phone.'

'Do you answer them all yourself?'

'Mostly. I would have answered a call at 11.30 a.m. definitely.'

Another office door opened and out came Juliet Gregg. She looked at Angel and smiled.

She was beautiful when she smiled. She was beautiful when she didn't smile.

'Good afternoon, Inspector Angel. Mr Twelvetrees is out; is there anything I can help you with?'

'Well, only a simple question, really,' he said.

She made a gesture with her hand, inviting him into her office.

Angel frowned. That was a bit unusual. He always dealt with Marcus Twelvetrees, never with her first-hand.

'Thank you,' he said. And he passed in front of her into a small outer office with a young lady at a desk tapping into a computer.

'Straight ahead, Inspector, keep going,' Juliet Gregg said from behind him.

Angel stepped forward through another open door. It revealed a spacious, oak-panelled room with two big windows. It was furnished with matching desk, table, chairs and bookshelves. Three framed certificates and several big oil paintings adorned the walls, and an open door beyond the built-in drinks bar indicated that the office also had the luxury of an adjoining bathroom.

He recalled what Marcus Twelvetrees had said to him at the al fresco party held there for her a week or so ago, that she would likely be fast-tracked to be a judge.

Juliet Gregg followed him in and sat down at her desk. She pointed to a chair opposite.

'Thank you,' he said, finding a comfortable, upholstered chair. 'I thought you might already have left to take up that partnership offer in Leeds.'

'I'm just working out my notice, Inspector, tying up loose ends and so on. I want to leave Marcus and the force with everything nice and tidy.'

He nodded and smiled. 'I was asking your receptionist, Tina, about a phone call here from a man called Norman Robinson last Friday. Do you remember such a call? It would probably have been from Glasgow.'

She pursed her lips briefly. 'No, I'm afraid not,' she said. 'Isn't that the name of the victim in the case you're working on?'

He looked up at her, surprised that she knew. She really was an eye-knocker. Her hair was jet black and shaped round her head like a prize chrysanthemum; her oval face framed her cheekbones, which were as high as a copper's helmet.

'I've been reading about it the newspapers,' she said. 'You've quite a reputation . . . an impressive record of success in criminal detection. They say you've solved every murder case you've ever worked on.'

He pulled a face. 'Oh yes,' he said. He sniffed noisily and added, 'They put me on a pedestal, so that when I fail to solve a case, they can enjoy knocking me off it.'

She began to laugh and looked across at him. He wasn't smiling.

She stopped laughing and said, 'I'm so sorry, Inspector. I didn't realize you were serious.'

'It's all right. To tell the truth I'm rather worried, Miss Gregg. Maybe they'll be knocking me off it quite soon. Criminals are getting smarter and smarter. But I don't have to tell you that. Do you know, I haven't got a clear motive nor an obvious suspect, yet.'

Still smiling, she said, 'Well, sorry I can't help you in this instance, Inspector, but I'm sure you'll get there in due course.'

'I certainly hope so,' he said as he got to his feet.

NINE

It was four o'clock when Angel arrived at the reception desk in the Feathers hotel. He was pleased that it was not busy. The duty manager was Mr Blacklock.

'Good afternoon, Inspector. Can I be of any help?'

'Yes, Mr Blacklock,' Angel said. 'I have reason to believe that there had been some flowers in room 201 last Sunday or early Monday morning. However, when our forensic team arrived, there was no sign of them, which is a mystery to us. We know that some of them were oriental lilies. Can you tell me anything about them . . . how they got there in the first place . . . who supplied them, what they were for, or what did they represent, and what happened to them?'

'Of course, Inspector. I'll just take a look,' Blacklock said, then he referred to a thick ledger already open on the counter in front of him. He began to turn back a few pages as he spoke. 'We don't put flowers in the rooms as a matter of course, Inspector. So many guests seem to have allergies. They don't suit everybody. But, of course, we would always supply them in advance of guests arriving, or have them delivered to specific requirements, if guests ordered them. We would keep a note of such disbursements in this journal, and a charge would subsequently be levied to the appropriate room account.' He arrived at the page he wanted. 'Let's see, now. It was Sunday last, the 2nd, wasn't it?' he said, running his finger down the column of entries. 'Mmm. There's nothing here, Inspector.'

Angel wasn't pleased. 'I don't suppose there was a delivery early Monday morning?'

Blacklock turned back to the journal. Eventually he looked up at him and said, 'No, Inspector. There were no deliveries of flowers or anything else to room 201 last Sunday or early on Monday morning, sorry.'

Angel frowned. 'Right. Thank you, Mr Blacklock,' he said as he turned away from the counter.

He couldn't get that smear of red pollen on the crisp white sheet of the dead man's bed out of his mind.

He pursed his lips.

He turned back to the counter.

Blacklock stepped forward. 'Yes, Inspector?'

'I'd like to have a quick word with one of your chambermaids, Monica Spalding, Mr Blacklock,' he said.

'Oh yes, of course,' Blacklock said as he reached out for the phone. 'She'll be on the first floor, Inspector. Please go up on the lift and I'll get her to meet you at the top.'

'Thank you,' Angel said.

The lift whizzed Angel up to the first floor and true to Blacklock's word, as the doors opened, there stood Monica Spalding.

Angel got out of the lift.

'You wanted me, Inspector,' she said, standing there, her hands shaking and her wide eyes flitting here and there.

Behind her were two smartly dressed men, edging to get into the lift. They pushed past her. Then a young couple came hurrying along the corridor also intent on catching the lift.

'I wanted to ask you a couple of questions, Monica. Can we go where we can talk?' Angel said.

She pulled up her keys which were on a chain, and opened the nearest bedroom door and showed him in. He looked round. The room was clean, smart and ready for occupation.

'Will this do?' she said, closing the door. 'We'll be all right here until the guest arrives.'

Angel nodded. 'This is fine,' he said. Then he turned back to face her. 'I am just checking about some flowers that may have been in room 201, last Sunday night, the night Norman Robinson was murdered. There is evidence that there were some flowers — oriental lilies actually — in the room. I wondered if you had seen anything of them.'

'No. No, I didn't see any flowers.'

'Did you remove any flowers to tidy up the place, because they were dead or for whatever reason, after you found the body?'

'No, Inspector. I've already told you that. I told you that when I realized he was dead, I just wanted to get away from him. I didn't take anything out of the room, flowers or anything else. I still don't like cleaning that room. It gives me the willies.'

Angel rubbed his chin. 'Sorry about that, Monica. I can understand that. Tell me, was it possible for anybody else to have removed anything — I'm thinking particularly of the flowers, but anything — from that room after you had found and reported the man dead?'

'No, Inspector,' she said. 'Definitely not.'

Angel blinked. 'What makes you so . . . positive?'

'Well, I didn't want anybody else to get the same shock I got when I found him like that, did I? So I hung about the lift door opposite 201 until your men arrived.'

'You're quite positive about that, Monica? You'd be quite prepared to say on oath in court that nobody entered the room between the time you reported finding him dead and when the forensic police team arrived?'

'Well, yes. But I hope I don't have to.'

'It probably won't be necessary, Monica, but you *may* have to.'

'Well, yes, I would.'

'Good. Thank you, Monica. That's all I wanted to know.'

There was a knock on the office door.

'Come in,' Angel called.

It was Ahmed. He was carrying several sheets of A4. 'I've finished checking off Johnson's calls, sir.'

Angel beamed. 'Ah yes, lad,' he said, 'you couldn't have come at a better time. What you got?'

'Well, Johnson isn't a big user of his mobile, sir. There are a few shops he has called and a local bookie. No family or women friends. The only number I couldn't properly fathom was a mobile number. Which he rang frequently, sometimes three times in a day, and so might be of interest, sir. I phoned the number and asked who they were and a man gave me a very frosty reply, so I said I had the wrong number and hung up.'

'Quite right. No need to arouse their suspicion.'

'I went through to the phone company, sir, and they say that it's not possible to trace the owner of the number because it is a "pay-as-you-go" phone.'

'Is that all, then?'

'That's the phone number at the bottom of the sheet.'

There was a knock at the door.

'Right, lad. See who that is, will you?'

Ahmed opened the door. It was DS Carter.

'Come on in, Flora,' Angel said. 'Ahmed was just leaving, weren't you?'

'Er, yes,' Ahmed said. He made a quick exit and closed the door.

Angel looked up at Flora and indicated a chair. She sat down.

'Now then, Flora, have you managed to organize it?' Angel asked.

'Yes, sir. I've had a new transmitting bug partnered to my mobile fitted to his mobile, and I have put it back in the envelope with the other stuff from his pockets in the charge room. He won't suspect a thing.'

'Let's hope so. You know what we want, anything that will indicate his involvement in the murder of Norman Robinson. All right?'

'I understand that, sir.'

Angel said, 'Now you can release Johnson. And remind him that he must keep his nose clean and that he will eventually be charged with resisting arrest, assaulting a police officer and damaging police property.'

'What about that £780 that was found in his house?'

'We can't prove it was stolen, so he's entitled to have it back,' Angel said, then he wrinkled his nose and added, 'for the time being.'

It was 8.28 a.m. Thursday morning, 6th June 2013.

The sun was shining. The birds were coughing. Police dogs were barking, and patrol car sirens could be heard racing up and down Bromersley in the police's perpetual bid to fight crime.

In the police station, Detective Inspector Angel was already in his office at his desk. He was gazing at the monstrous pot ornament and still wondering what animal it was or what it represented. He moved it from the top of his growing pile of post and reports, and began fingering through the envelopes.

There was a knock at the door. It was DS Crisp.

'Good morning, sir,' he said.

'Ah. You're back from haggis land, lad. Good. I've got another urgent job for you.'

Crisp frowned. 'I've a lot of paperwork to catch up, sir. And I've to sort out my expenses.'

Then his eye caught the pot monster on the desk.

'And, erm, what's that, sir, a new paperweight?'

'What, lad? Oh that. It's a figure in fine china.'

'Can I pick it up, sir?'

Angel passed it to him.

Crisp looked at the head thoroughly, then its stomach and then its feet. 'Is it a gorilla on all fours?' he said. 'They always look a bit odd. Or a reindeer? Hmmm. Very . . . er, smart, sir,' he said, placing it back on the desk.

'Would you like it for your desk, Trevor?'

'Oh no, sir. Thank you.'

'For your mantelpiece at home?'

'Looks very good on your desk, sir. What sort of animal is it?'

Angel clenched his fists. 'I don't know,' he snapped. 'Let's get on.'

He brought Crisp up to date with the Robinson murder and explained how they had discovered that the murderer had brought oriental lilies to the scene.

He continued, 'So I want you to call on all the florists and places where they sell flowers nearest to the Feathers between 5.10 p.m., the time the train came in, and 6.00 p.m., when he arrived at the Feathers. There can't be many places that were open on a Sunday. It's absolutely vital. There may have been other flowers included in the bunch or bouquet. But whoever bought those lilies is the murderer, so we need a full description of him. All right?'

Crisp screwed up his face and shook his head. 'It's a long shot, sir,' he said.

Angel said. 'I know it's a long shot. But this is a difficult case. Now, buzz off and get on with it.'

Crisp wasn't best pleased. He went out and closed the door.

Angel watched him go and shook his head, then reached out to the pile and pulled it towards him. He was about to open an envelope when the phone went. He reached out for it.

It was Superintendent Harker. 'I've just had a triple nine. A man has been found dead in a first-floor bedroom of the King George hotel on Main Street. Reported in by the manageress, Mrs Vermont.'

Angel's heart began to thump. His chest was on fire. 'Right, sir,' he said, but Harker had already hung up.

Angel rang DS Taylor of SOCO, then Dr Mac, then Inspector Haydn Asquith, then DS Carter.

Then, when he had chance to think, he realized that on the face of it, there were similarities to the Robinson case: man's body found dead in a hotel. He was anxious to find out all the details of the man's death, but he must give SOCO time to make the initial scientific inspection of the site unhindered. The uncontaminated forensic evidence they might uncover could save him weeks of work, and perhaps produce an easy conviction.

He then busied himself with attempting to reduce the pile in front of him and made a little progress.

About an hour later, his phone rang. He snatched it up. It was Don Taylor ringing from the crime scene at the King George.

'Right, Don, what have you got?'

'You're not going to like this, sir.'

Angel's face muscles tightened. He sighed and said, 'Spit it out, Don. What is it?'

'We've got a body, male, sir, aged about fifty or fifty-five, name of Patrick Novak, found in a bedroom on a very disturbed bed, half-dressed, staring eyes, just like Norman Robinson. Something else — you won't believe, sir — there's a fruit gum on the carpet at the side of the bed.'

Angel blinked, shook his head . . . then rubbed his chin. 'Anything else?' he said.

'Dr Mac wants a word, sir.'

'Put him on, Don.'

'Mac here. Yes. It looks like a repeat of the Robinson case, Michael, except this victim is about thirty years older.'

'Are you ready for me yet?' Angel said. He was anxious to get to the scene and see the situation for himself.

'Come on over, Michael, I'll be ready for moving the body in a few minutes.'

'Right, Mac. I'll be about ten minutes.'

Angel cancelled the call and left his office as it was. Closing the door, he looked into the CID office, caught DS Carter's eye, and twelve minutes later they were travelling upwards in the rickety lift of the King George hotel. Angel noticed the absence of CCTV cameras in the lift and along the corridors.

The clunking and rattling stopped. They were at the first floor.

It was easy to find the room they wanted.

A uniformed policeman was standing at the door of room 114. He recognized Angel, saluted, knocked on the door, turned the handle and pushed it open.

'Thank you,' Angel said, as he and Flora went into the room.

It was a small single bedroom, decorated in wallpaper fashionable in 1949 and furnished with odds and ends from archaic workhouses.

Angel wrinkled his nose.

There were three SOCO men in whites. One was taking photographs of everything that didn't move, another was on his hands and knees under the bed, and another, Don Taylor, was removing the dust-collecting unit from a powerful vacuum, transferring it to an evidence bag, sealing it and entering the sector it had swept and the present time and date.

Dr Mac, also in whites, was on his knees at the side of the bed, packing an anal thermometer into a sleeve and putting that into a large bag.

Don Taylor looked up, and acknowledged Angel and DS Carter.

'Good morning, sir. Good morning, Flora,' he said, and he put his pen in his pocket as he walked up to them.

'Have you finished the sweep and the vacuum, Don?'

'Yes, sir,' Taylor said. 'And Dr Mac's ready to have the body moved.'

'I am that, Michael,' Mac said, looking up.

'Right. Won't keep you, Mac,' Angel said as he approached the bed.

He saw the body of a man crouched in a foetal position. He was dark-haired going grey, about fifty or sixty, his eyes were open, apparently staring into space. He was wearing only a shirt, vest and socks. The buttons on his shirt were undone. The bed was in great disorder, the blankets, sheets and pillows strewn about in a chaotic fashion.

'No sign of any lipstick on this man, Mac?' Angel said.

'Couldn't see any,' the doctor said. 'Have you seen all you want to see of him, Michael?'

'Oh yes, Mac. Thank you.'

The doctor nodded, then turned away, took out his mobile and began to make a call.

Angel saw a white chalk mark on the carpet just under the edge of the bed. It was there to indicate a shiny red fruit gum.

He looked at Taylor. 'Is that fruit gum exactly the same as we found under Norman Robinson's bed, Don?'

'It certainly looks like it, sir.'

'No sign of the bag or packet anywhere? In his pockets or the wastepaper basket?'

'No, sir.'

'Hmm. It means — like the Robinson case — it must have been brought in by the murderer.' He turned to DS Carter. 'Make a note of that, Flora.'

'Right, sir,' she said, pulling out her notebook and fumbling in her pocket for a pen.

Angel looked round the room . . . the wardrobe . . . chest of drawers . . . luggage stand with small case on it . . . ancient washbasin with mirror above it . . . window looking out onto the back of the box factory . . . bedside locker and a chair at the other side of the bed with the rest of the dead man's clothes thrown onto it.

He turned back to look at Taylor. 'Any sign that they had been drinking?' he said.

'Yes, sir. There are marks where glasses and a bottle have stood on the white porcelain shelf above the washbasin. It is detachable, so we are taking the shelf with us. In the lab, I'll be able to completely dry the shelf, then maybe get a photograph of the marks left. They might match the marks left by the glasses and the bottle found on the bedside cabinet from the Feathers.'

Angel squeezed the lobe of his ear between finger and thumb. 'It would be good if they *did* match, Don. What else have you got?'

Taylor referred to the clipboard he had been carrying.

'As far as we know, sir, his name is Patrick Novak, aged — at a guess — in his late fifties. Apparently he lives at 12, Lilac Avenue, Coalsden, Norwich. He has more than £100 cash on him, a credit card, and a second-class return rail ticket to Norwich. He has a bunch of keys on him, but no car key. Also he doesn't seem to have a mobile phone. He arrived last night about six o'clock, having booked in for one night. He was found by Mrs Vermont, the landlady, at 8.30 this morning. This hotel has no CCTV, neither upstairs nor down, so no joy there; it's a pub with rooms to let, really. There is a door from the back yard, which has space for a dozen or so cars to park. Entrance to the rooms can be made either from the front to the bar, then through a door that says, "Residents Only", or through the back door past the reception office. However, there's nobody on reception after eight o'clock at night until 7.30 a.m. The back door is unlocked until after they've locked up the pub, which would be about eleven o'clock. Hmm . . . and I think that's about it, sir.'

Angel rubbed his chin. 'Any signs of any flowers . . . oriental lilies . . . pollen on the bed sheets . . . anything like that?'

'No, sir,' Taylor said.

Angel frowned. 'So there are differences,' he muttered, chiefly to himself. Then he turned to DS Carter and said, 'Have you got that down, Flora?'

'Yes, sir,' she said. Then, looking at her notes, she said, 'There are no signs of flowers, therefore there are differences.'

'Good,' he said. 'While I think about it, get me Trevor Crisp on the phone.'

Flora nodded, took out her mobile and tapped in a number.

Angel turned back to Taylor. 'Did Novak bring any luggage with him?'

'A small, cheap suitcase. There's nothing in it — only a shirt, pyjamas and his washing tackle.'

'I shall want to see it all and the contents of his pockets, Don, as soon as you can.'

Mac had finished his call. He put the mobile in his pocket and came up to Angel. 'The meat wagon's on its way,' he said.

Angel nodded. 'Right, Mac. What have you got?'

The old doctor said, 'The man was poisoned, Michael, probably a carbon copy of the Norman Robinson murder, and if you want my opinion the murderer will most certainly be a woman. No man would want to put anyone through as much pain as these two men will have suffered. As with Robinson, this man would have been in acute pain, then fallen into a coma and then died. Of course, I will have to confirm this after I have done all my tests.'

'Excuse me, sir,' Flora said. 'There's no reply from Trevor Crisp's mobile.'

Angel wasn't pleased. He breathed in and then out noisily. 'No,' he said, 'there never is! Will you keep trying?'

'It keeps sending me to voicemail,' she said.

'All right. Leave it for now.'

He turned back to Mac. 'Sorry about that, Mac. Do you know that lad is harder to find than the Lost Chord.'

Mac smiled, then shook his head. 'You're so impatient, Michael.'

'You don't know. He is always missing. Now, where was I? Oh yes, have you calculated the time of death?'

'Aye. It would have been between eight o'clock and midnight last night.'

'That was the same time you said for Norman Robinson.'

The doctor nodded. 'Aye, I did.'

'Right, Mac. Thank you,' Angel said and then he turned to Taylor. 'Do you know if he ate anything here since he arrived?'

'Don't know, sir. No signs in here of a takeaway brought in or dirty pots from room service or anything like that,' Taylor said.

Angel nodded. 'Right. What was the name of the woman who found him?'

'The manageress, Mrs Vermont. She's downstairs in reception waiting for you.'

'Right, Don,' he said. 'Thank you.' He turned to Flora and said, 'Come on, lass.'

TEN

Angel knocked on the door marked *Reception Office*.

'Come in,' a woman's voice called.

Angel opened the door and walked into the tiny office followed by Flora Carter, who took out her notebook and pen in anticipation.

He saw the woman seated at a desk. She looked at him with a sort of smile. He had seen a more convincing smile on a tiger.

'Mrs Vermont?' Angel said.

'I suppose you are the famous Inspector Angel, come to ask me about Mr Novak,' she said. 'I am very pleased to meet you. Please sit down, both of you.'

She was a big woman of about sixty. She had a plunging neckline, wore too much make-up and too much jewellery. She rattled whenever she moved. The noise came from either the pendants hanging from the silver chains she wore round her neck, or the heavy silver charm bracelet that graced her thick wrist, or both in unison.

Angel said, 'Thank you, Mrs Vermont. I understand that you found the dead man, Patrick Novak, in room 114?'

'I did indeed, Inspector.'

'Tell me, how did you come to find him?'

'Well, he had asked for a call at 8.15 a.m., so I knocked on his door several times but didn't get any reply. I left it for about five minutes and had another go. There was still no reply. I banged on the door a third time and called out, without result. I was beginning to be worried. Eventually I called out that I was coming in. I got out my pass key, but I needn't have bothered. The door wasn't locked. I opened it, peered into the room. I saw him curled up on the bed. I called out, "Your early call, Mr Novak, it's 8.25 a.m." He didn't move. I went over to the bed and shook his shoulder. He was cold and as stiff as a board. I knew he was dead. I came straight out of the room and rushed down here and phoned 999.'

'Apart from the dead man's shoulder and the door handle, you didn't touch anything else in the room?'

'No, I don't believe I touched the door handle inside, Inspector, because when I went in, I didn't close the door. You have to remember that although I am manageress of the hotel I am a woman,' she said, pulling in her stomach and sticking out her big bosom and waggling her shoulders alternately, 'and I wouldn't want any of my guests to get the wrong idea.'

Angel glanced at Flora and stifled a smile. 'Of course, Mrs Vermont. Excuse me, I wasn't thinking.'

She looked at him demurely.

Angel quickly looked away. 'Did you see him with anybody during the short time he was here?'

'I'm afraid I didn't see anything of him after I booked him in. Not until I saw his body this morning.'

'You didn't notice if there were any flowers in his room? I am thinking in particular, of oriental lilies.'

She looked at him with a very blank face. 'Oriental lilies? No.'

'Did Mr Novak eat anything here at all?'

She puffed out her bosom and said, 'I hope you are not suggesting that his death was the result of anything he ate here, Inspector Angel?'

'No, no, my dear lady. Of course not. We think that we know how he died, but I need to know everything I can about him . . . particularly the last few hours of his life.'

She lowered the bosom. 'Oh, I see. No, as a matter of fact, he didn't dine here. The dining room closes at eight o'clock. I don't know what he did about a meal. I didn't see him leave or return.'

'Perhaps he intended dining somewhere else later . . . Incidentally, there was a fruit gum found on the bedroom floor, Mrs Vermont. Have you any idea how it got there?'

'A fruit gum? Well, no. It wouldn't have been there when he arrived. Mr Novak must have brought it with him.'

'Yes. But there weren't any others in his pockets, and there was no empty box or bag anywhere in the room.'

She shook her head. 'Sorry, Inspector, can't explain it, then.'

Angel rubbed his chin. 'Who cleans the rooms and prepares them for the guests?'

'I do. I do almost everything to do with this side of the business. My husband runs the bars with a cook and two part-time girls, and I run the accommodation side with occasional help.'

'Are you certain that the fruit gum was not there before Mr Novak arrived?'

She looked downwards thoughtfully. 'Positive. If such a thing had been there, I am certain that the vacuum would have picked it up.'

'And you didn't empty the wastepaper basket, after you found the dead man this morning?'

'No.'

'Mrs Vermont, if Mr Novak had been visited by a friend, and wanted to entertain him or her, could he have ordered a bottle of wine, say, and two tumblers to be delivered to his room?'

'Well yes, he could have, Inspector, but he didn't. But if he had, he would have had to order it from me and I would have phoned through to the bar and asked my husband to send one of the barmaids up to the room with a tray.'

'But you're not available after eight o'clock.'

'That's quite correct. Room service finishes at eight o'clock. However, after then, he could have ordered it from the bar and signed for it in person, but that didn't happen either. A chitty would have come through to me from the bar to go onto his bill.'

'Yes, I see. Thank you. About booking the room . . . did he write to you or phone you to book the room?'

'He telephoned, Inspector. I took the call on Tuesday morning, I think it was.'

'Can you remember anything about the call?'

'No. I don't think so. Just a straightforward booking for the following night, Wednesday night. I realized when he gave his address as near Norwich that he spoke with that lovely Norfolk drawl.'

Angel blinked. He turned to DS Carter and said, 'Flora, be sure to make a note of that. The victim, in this case, wasn't a local man. Apparently he came from Norfolk.'

Flora Carter nodded knowingly. 'Right, sir,' she said.

Angel turned back to Mrs Vermont. 'And who booked him in on his arrival?' he said.

'I did. There's only me.'

'How did he strike you?'

She shook her head and gave a shrug.

Angel blinked. 'There was nothing at all unusual about him?' he said.

'No. Not that I recall.'

'Was he chewing anything, for instance?'

'No, I don't think so. I never noticed anything special about him, Inspector, except for his accent.'

'His unmistakable Norfolk drawl,' Angel said, rubbing his chin. 'Right, Mrs Vermont. That's all for now. Thank you.'

There was a knock on Angel's office door. It was Ahmed.

'You wanted me, sir?'

'I've been trying to get DS Crisp, lad. I don't suppose you know where he is?'

Ahmed frowned. 'He's not in the CID office, sir. I haven't seen him all day.'

Angel's lips tightened back against his teeth. He rubbed his chin rapidly. 'Drop everything and find him for me. Flora and I have been trying to reach him on his mobile. I sent him off circulating local florists. I don't know where the hell he has disappeared to.'

Angel's mobile rang. 'Find him for me, Ahmed,' he said as he pulled the phone out of his pocket.

'Right, sir,' said Ahmed and he went out.

Angel saw from the LCD on his mobile that it was his wife, Mary, calling. He pressed the button and said, 'Yes, love, what is it?'

'Oh. Have I caught you at a bad time?' she said.

'I'm at work, love. Are you all right?'

'Well, erm, yes. I've had a phone call from Mrs Mackenzie. Now, you know what an awful time charities are having? Well, the Summer Ball in Muick Castle was such a big success that she wants to hold another event as soon as she possibly can. And she's had a word with Lady Muick, and she proposes to make it a fancy-dress do. The date she has chosen is a week on Saturday, the 15th. Now, as you know, I'm on the committee so I'll have to help and support her. I just wanted to make sure that you'll be free on that date. I don't want to go without you.'

'Well yes, love. I suppose I will be. But you know how things are in this job.'

'Yes . . . well, I just hope nothing untoward happens on *that* night. I'm giving you lots of notice. Put it in your diary. I'll have to find a fancy dress for you.'

'All right. I will. I will. I'll put it in straightaway. Saturday, 15th. Fancy-Dress Ball at Muick Castle. Don't make that costume for me too ridiculous.'

'Right, love. Thank you. That's all.'

'All right, sweetheart. Goodbye.'

Angel replaced the phone. He wondered what Mrs Mackenzie was going to do about security. Perhaps Lady Muick could be persuaded not to wear the necklace.

He looked in the directory for Mrs Mackenzie's number and phoned her. He made the point about security strongly to her.

'But her ladyship insists on wearing it, Inspector,' Mrs Mackenzie said. 'She says the people expect her to wear it. She is the only nobility in the town. She couldn't go to a dress occasion such as I am planning looking like a drudge. However, have no fear. Whatever plans we make we will remember all the points you have made. Thank you very much. Goodbye.'

Angel knew when he had been given the bum's rush. But there was nothing further he could do.

He pulled the pile of post towards him and began filtering through the letters as his phone rang. He snatched it up. 'Angel,' he said.

It was Ahmed.

'I've found DS Crisp, sir. He's just pulled onto the car park. He'll be with you directly.'

'Right, lad,' Angel said and he banged down the phone.

He sat back in his chair, breathing heavily, his face muscles tight. He silently rehearsed what he wanted to say to him.

A few seconds passed and there was a knock at the door.

'Come in,' Angel roared.

It was Crisp. The sergeant came in all bright-eyed and full of enthusiasm. He began to speak as soon as he got through the door.

'I've found the shop, sir,' he said. 'It's that scruffy little lock-up greengrocer's on the corner of Station Road and Main Street, a cock-stride from the rail station,' he said as he closed the door. 'It's underneath that fancy-dress hire place, where you can hire costumes from Elvis Presley to King Henry VIII.'

'What's the name of the shopkeeper?'

'Enoch Truelove, sir. They don't sell many flowers but they usually have a few made-up bunches in the window. It's a shop that sells everything and is open all hours. Mr Truelove said he remembered selling a man half a dozen lilies on Sunday. And, what's more, he said that he thought he might recognize the man if he was to see him again.'

Angel frowned. 'A man? You're sure he said a man?'

'Positive, sir.'

The lines on Angel's forehead became more defined. 'Would a man buy another man flowers? Particularly lilies?'

Crisp grinned. 'Not unless they were dating, sir.'

He looked at Crisp knowingly. 'I suppose many men like flowers. I like some flowers, but I would never think of buying another man flowers, and I wouldn't be really that pleased if a man bought *me* flowers.'

Crisp smiled. 'Are we dealing with the phenomenon of a man who wanted to be a woman, sir?'

'I don't know,' Angel said. 'I simply don't know.'

He remembered that they had found lipstick on the dead man's lips. It had been explained away by the suggestion that the murderer was a woman and that they had kissed. It wasn't beyond the realms of possibility, and Angel had not dismissed the idea.

'I wouldn't want to be a woman,' Crisp said.

'We're not talking about us, lad,' he said. 'Anyway, I'll go and have a word with Mr Truelove myself. In the meantime, I want you to go to Norwich.'

'Norwich?' Crisp said.

Angel updated him and told him that he wanted him to look into the background of Patrick Novak, to see what similarities — if any — existed between the two victims. He reckoned that that could greatly assist his investigation into their murders.

'Right, sir,' Crisp said, then he looked at his watch. 'I'll have to see what time the trains leave for Norwich tomorrow.'

'Take your issued car, lad, it'll be quicker.'

Crisp frowned. 'It's a long way, sir. I must set off first thing in the morning.'

'You can nip home now, pack a bag and be off in less than half an hour,' Angel said.

'But sir, I need to find a place to stay and then I have to find my way round. I could do all that tomorrow and be ready to start on Saturday.'

'Aye. And that's the weekend, lad. You've a satnav to find your way around, and a phone call will soon get you booked into a hotel. It's about a three-hour drive. You can be there by six o'clock. I'll phone you in the morning . . . see what you've managed to find out.'

Crisp wasn't pleased. He turned towards the door.

Angel said, 'Just a minute, lad. Where have you been this last twenty-four hours, and what's wrong with your mobile?'

Crisp turned back. He assumed a most innocent look. 'There's nothing wrong with my mobile, sir, as far as I know. Ahmed phoned me a few minutes ago. It's working all right.'

Angel ran his hand through his hair. 'Well, keep the damned thing switched on. How else can I keep in touch with you?'

'I never switch it off in working hours, sir.'

'But it was switched off!'

Crisp frowned. 'Well, I don't understand it.'

'I do. Keep the bloody thing switched on all the time, so that I can contact you. Where were you anyway?'

'I've been very busy, sir. With a different case. There was a posh old-time dance in the ballroom at the Feathers, and the women's powder room was systematically searched and robbed. Also at one point, the lights in the ballroom went out and in the darkness two ladies had their valuable necklaces stolen.'

'Didn't they feel them go?'

'They heard the snip of a pair of pliers, felt them whisked off their necks, but they couldn't see who took them. It all happened so quickly.'

'Who was there?'

'Everybody who is anybody. You know, sir, the usual mob.'

'Lady Muick, Mrs Mackenzie, Sir Rodney Stamp . . .'

'Oh yes, sir. All of them. By the way, young Stewart Twelvetrees asked after you and sent his good wishes.'

'That was kind of him. I expect he was there with his wife, Lydia, and her sister, Nadine?'

'Oh yes, sir. All of that brigade. And his dad, Twelvetrees Senior, and that sexy Juliet Gregg woman.'

'Any suspects, lad?'

'There was nothing to go on, sir. The place was searched from top to bottom but nothing was found. And it was a bit difficult dealing with la crème de la crème.'

'There's no difficulty at all, lad. They're exactly the same as us except they've got more money, and can pay their gas bill without worrying about it, that's all.'

Crisp shrugged. Then he noticed the pot monster on the desk and took the opportunity to change the subject. 'Got a new paperweight, sir?'

Angel nodded.

'What is it?' Crisp said. 'Is it a centaur, half human and half horse? Very smart, if you're into that sort of thing.'

Angel looked at him.

'No, it isn't,' Crisp said. 'It's a Cyclops. No it can't be. It's got three eyes. A Cyclops only has one eye, doesn't it, sir?'

Angel continued to look at him.

Crisp frowned. 'I know, sir. It's one of the creatures in *Dr Who*, isn't it?'

Angel blinked. 'Is it?' he said.

'I'm not sure.'

'Do you watch *Dr Who*, lad?'

'No, sir. Not now. I used to.'

Angel smiled. 'Would you like it, to remind you of those days?'

'Oh no, sir. No, thank you.'

Angel wrinkled his nose.

Angel pointed the bonnet of the BMW in the direction of the railway station until he reached a scruffy little greengrocer's lock-up shop, on the corner of Station Road and Main Street.

He saw a sign above the window that read 'Enoch Truelove — Greengrocers' and a smaller sign plugged into the wall and pointing upwards to a staircase, which read, 'Fancy-Dress Hire — 1st Floor.'

He parked right outside the front of the greengrocer's shop. He pushed open the old shop door. A bell on a large coil sprang up and down and rang above his head. As he closed the door, it rang some more.

An elderly man in shirtsleeves, khaki shorts and a well-worn straw hat came shuffling up to a doorway three steps higher than the floor of the shop. He stopped at the doorway, looked down on Angel and said, 'And what can I get for you, young man?'

'Mr Enoch Truelove?'

The old man looked over his glasses and said, 'Yes. Who wants to know?'

'DI Angel, Bromersley police,' he said, offering his ID card.

Truelove came quickly down the steps, ignored the ID card and looked Angel up and down.

Angel said, 'I'm following up the inquiries my sergeant made about the man who bought a bunch of flowers from you — oriental lilies — on Sunday last.'

'Oh yes,' he said. 'What about them? There was nothing wrong with them, was there? They were fresh. They were only delivered from the wholesalers that morning. You can't come making a complaint about them four days after they were sold. I mean, I sold them in good faith.'

'As far as I know, Mr Truelove, the flowers were fine.'

'I even knocked a few pence off because the man said that that was all the money he'd got on him.'

Angel rubbed his chin. Something occurred to him, something rather odd. Don Taylor had said that Robinson had no cash on him either, not a coin. But Robinson was the victim, not the murderer. It could, of course, be that the murderer went through Robinson's pockets and had taken all his money, because the murderer was penniless!

'Mr Truelove, you said you knocked a few pence off the cost of the flowers?'

'Yes, I did.'

'Can you tell me how that came about?'

'Of course. He wanted a bunch of flowers for his girlfriend, he said. I only had the bunch of lilies left, and they were six pounds. He said, could he look at them, so I took them out of the window and gave them to him. He looked at them. I could see he wanted them. He asked me how much they were and I said six pounds. He opened his wallet and took out a five-pound note. I could see that he only had the one fiver in there, no other notes. Then he rummaged about in his pocket and pulled out a few coins. He looked at them and they came to sixty-something pence. He looked up at me shyly and asked me if I'd take that instead of the full pound because he hadn't any more. Well, I don't like bartering with customers, you know, Inspector, and he seemed to be genuine so I said all right.'

Angel nodded. 'Right. Thank you,' he said. He rubbed his chin. He had an idea.

'Was that helpful, Inspector?' Truelove said.

'It was,' he said. 'Tell me, Mr Truelove, would you recognize the man if I showed you a photograph of him?'

'I think so.'

'I'll be back later.'

Angel was delighted. He came out of the shop as if he was floating on air. He couldn't get in the car fast enough. He dialled up the number of the mortuary and asked to speak to Dr Mac.

'Yes, Michael,' the Glaswegian said.

'Ah, Mac. I've maybe got a man who can identify Norman Robinson. Now I know he's been in the wars and whatever, but can you make him look presentable enough to be photographed head and shoulders and shown to a witness?'

'I don't know, Michael. The lines on the man's face will be much more pronounced than they were when he was alive, and his eyes will still be staring in that unrealistic way, that could disturb some people.'

'You can close his eyelids, can't you?'

'I could for the purposes of a photograph, yes.'

'If you think it will look better, please do that. And powder his face. That'll soften the hardness of the wrinkles.'

'Yes. I can do that as well.'

'I'm sending a chap from SOCO to take the photograph. He should be with you in about a quarter of an hour. Is that OK?'

'I'll be ready for him.'

'Thanks, Mac.'

Angel then tapped in the number of Don Taylor at SOCO and arranged for the photograph to be taken ASAP and brought straight to his office.

Then he drove the BMW back to the station.

ELEVEN

Angel arrived at his office a few minutes later to find a large brown 'Evidence' envelope on his desk. The label stuck onto it advised him that it contained the personal effects of Patrick Novak and that it had come from the SOCO's office for his attention.

He quickly sat down, opened the seal and carefully poured the contents onto his desk.

There was a leather wallet that had £100 in £20 notes, a return rail ticket to Norwich, a folded newspaper cutting and a tiny photograph of a very young baby, apparently taken while in a hospital incubator.

Angel frowned as he turned the photograph back over and gazed at it. It seemed to be a very small baby. It had a plastic mask across its nose and mouth fastened with sticky tape to the cheeks with a length of piping leading from it, a tiny attachment to an ear with a thin wire leading from it, another attachment concealed by bandages to the baby's chest with a thin wire leading from it and another wire or tube attached to the foot. The photograph was fuzzy and slightly out of focus. Angel turned it over. In pencil on the back was scrawled, 'May 2nd, 2002'.

He put it back in the wallet and opened the newspaper cutting. It turned out to be the top half of the front page of the *News Chronicle*. He opened it up. It read:

Fruit-gum sucker poisons man

A man has been murdered in a three-star luxury Hotel in the South Yorkshire market town of Bromersley. The victim has been identified as Norman Robinson, 28, late of Canal Street, Bromersley, recently living in Glasgow. The only clues the police have are a fruit gum and pollen from oriental lilies which were left at the scene of the murder. The victim, Norman Robinson, was a popular young man who had been training as a chef. His father had been a maintenance engineer for Bromersley Council. Head of the investiga-tion is Detective Inspector Angel, head of homicide in Bromersley. He has become famous for solving many puzzling murders including the barefoot murders in 2003 and the umbrella murders in 2006.

Angel was rereading the cutting when there was a knock at the door. 'Come in.'

It was a detective constable from SOCO. 'I've brought the post-mortem photographs of Norman Robinson, sir.'

He handed Angel four postcard-size photographs, all four slightly different computer printouts of the head and shoulders of the dead man.

Then the DC's eyes alighted on the monster ornament on Angel's desk.

'My, that's a remarkable model animal, sir. What is it?' he said.

'I don't know, lad,' Angel said without looking up. His attention was on the photographs; he was studying each one in turn.

The DC was still looking at the monster, but he said, 'Are they all right, sir? I tried the light in different positions to try to minimize the hardness of the corpse's wrinkles.'

'Aye. They're great. I think I'll use the one with the light on full-frontal. Thank you for closing his eyes and powdering him up. He looks almost human.'

'That wasn't me, sir, that was Dr Mac,' the DC said and then he added, 'I didn't know you were into modern art, sir. Some works of art sell for thousands.'

Angel blinked. 'Do you reckon that animal in best china is in that category?'

'It's not what I think, sir. It's a matter of what the market decides. Personally I think it's hideous, sir, but what do I know?'

He turned to go. He looked back. 'I hope that photograph fits the bill, sir.'

Angel nodded. 'Thank you, lad.'

The DC went out and closed the door.

Angel picked up the monster and glared at it. It didn't matter whichever way he looked at it, it was ugly. He pulled a face and quickly put it down on the desk. Then, armed with the photograph, he went straight out of the station and into the BMW. He started the engine and headed towards Enoch Truelove's shop.

Angel handed Enoch Truelove the photograph. The old man took it to the shop window for more light. 'Yes. That's the man, Inspector,' he said.

Angel rubbed his chin. 'That's the man who bought a bunch of white oriental lilies from you last Sunday teatime?'

'Yes. And he didn't quite have enough money.'

'And so you let him off a few bob?'

'I thought the girl must be very special for him to spend his last penny on her.'

Angel's face creased. He was going to have to change his mindset. At the beginning of this investigation, he had instinctively assumed that the murderer was a man. But now it looked as if Truelove's evidence turned that assumption upside down.

Truelove said: 'Most customers are, what you might say, reluctant customers. They don't want to spend anything. And when they see something at a price they might be willing to pay they start bargaining with you, trying to get it even cheaper.'

'Would you be prepared to go into the witness box and swear before a judge and jury that that was the man?'

'Oh, I haven't time for that, Inspector. I've a business to run. Who would mind the shop while I went to court?'

'You wouldn't want the man's murderer to get away free, would you?'

The old man looked at Angel with a pained expression on his face.

Angel returned to the BMW and went to the town's general hospital on Carlton Road. He was lucky to find a convenient parking spot. He went through the main door, where he turned left, then right, along a very long corridor to the mortuary at the end. As usual, the door was closed and locked. He rang the bell and eventually was admitted by a man in blue overalls and green wellington boots. He was shown into Dr Mac's little office, which had internal glass windows overlooking an operating theatre. The outline of a body covered by a white sheet was on a table. The smell was horrible and too awful for words.

Dr Mac looked up from his computer screen. 'Come in, Michael. This is a surprise. What brings you up here?' he said.

'How you work in this stink is beyond me.' Angel said.

'It's your fault, laddie. If you didn't keep finding dead bodies, we could soon hose the place down, open the windows and have it permanently smelling of heather and wild thistles.'

Angel shook his head and smiled.

Mac said, 'Anyway, what are you wanting? I have just finished the examination of the body of Patrick Novak, if that's what you're about?'

Angel's eyebrows shot up. 'Good. Anything unusual?'

'Not as far as I'm concerned. Novak was poisoned in the same way, and to approximately the same degree, as Norman Robinson. There's nothing else that I think will cause you to raise an eyebrow, Michael. I'll email my report to you later this afternoon.'

'Thanks, Mac,' he said. He thought a moment and then said, 'Two men, murdered in hotels with the same poison, by a woman.'

'A woman now, you say?'

'I think so,' he said with a decisive nod. 'The only clues: marks of a bottle and two glasses, and a fruit gum. What's the point of the fruit gum, Mac?'

'Does there have to be a point to it? Maybe she just likes fruit gums.'

Angel said. 'Nobody goes around poisoning a man, thoroughly cleans up all the evidence but allows a fruit gum to be left behind. It's not as if it is the sign of the Mafia or a triad or something.'

Mac shook his head. 'Fruit gums only show the sign of a man or woman with a sweet tooth,' he said.

'You must be right, Mac. A woman who likes fruit gums.'

'Let me ask you, Michael. Have you got anybody in the frame for these murders?'

'Well, not seriously. If it's a woman, I may very well have to look closely at Michelle Brown from Glasgow. She was the partner of Norman Robinson. It might be seen that she had a motive. Norman leaves her, comes south to collect some money to take back up there. He doesn't tell her who he is collecting it from. At the same time, she is getting angry with him because she believes he has another woman in tow. You never know what other skeletons there are in her cupboard.'

'Anybody else?'

'No. Not yet. And that's if it is a woman. Now, if it turns out to be a man, then it must be Thomas Johnson. In the case of Norman Robinson, he was in the Feathers on the night of the murder, and he's a thoroughly bad lot. He was also found in possession of the same fruit gums that were found by both victims.'

'I see,' the old doctor said.

'If only I understood why a fruit gum was found at each of the crime scenes. Any ideas, Mac?'

'No, laddie, no. I'm afraid I canna help you with your sweeties just now. Now, if you have anything forensic or scientific, I might be able to help.'

Angel smiled. 'As a matter of fact there is something,' he said as he took out his wallet. 'It's your advice I want as an obstetrician now. That was one of your roles in a previous life, wasn't it?'

'Aye, and happy days they were, although I had to leave Glasgow and move east to the strange folk of Edinburgh to get my degree.'

Angel grinned. He opened the wallet and out of one of the small pockets he produced a small photograph and handed it to him. 'I found that in Patrick Novak's wallet,' he said. 'I have no idea who it is. What can you tell me about it?'

Mac licked his lips, peered at it and said, 'It was taken by an amateur, in a bad light with a cheap camera. I can tell you that.'

'I daresay. But what can you tell me about the baby?'

The doctor looked at it a little while before he spoke.

'I would say firstly that this looks like the bairn is in a hospital incubator, and is very underweight and extremely young. I am inclined to suggest that it is only a day or two old and is premature by between thirty and fifty days. It would have been, or should have been, in intensive care, judging by the need for a mask. It obviously had breathing difficulties. Also, at the time, it was being monitored for oxygen saturation and the checking of its blood. I reckon the bairn was in pretty bad shape. The photograph not being in colour, I am unable to offer any other concrete observation.'

'Thank you, Mac. That might be very helpful. Is there anything there to indicate the child's sex?'

'No,' he said as he turned the photograph over and looked at the date pencilled on the back. 'May 2nd, 2002,' he said. He looked up at Angel. 'Is that the date of the photograph?'

'I expect so, Mac. What do you think?'

'Aye. I think it most probably is. If it was, the child would be eleven years old now. Who do you know, connected with this case, who has a child of eleven?'

'Nobody. It's probably one of Patrick Novak's. I've that to find out.'

'Good luck with that, Michael.'

Angel wrinkled his face. 'Aye. Well, thank you. I need as much luck as I can get.'

It was Friday morning, 7th June.

Angel was in his office early. He was trying to make a reduction in the pile of accumulated post and internal mail on his desk. He was engrossed in a complex pamphlet written by a prosecuting barrister about the status of the police called to a domestic incident between a woman and her bed-sharing partner, where the bed-sharing partner was a serving police officer. It was just getting to the interesting part when there was a knock on the door.

He wrinkled his nose. He looked up. 'Come in,' he called.

It was Don Taylor.

'What is it, lad?' he said, closing the pamphlet.

'Good morning, sir,' Taylor said. 'I have just completed tests comparing the marks made by the two glasses and the bottle on the bedside cabinet we took from the Feathers hotel with the marks on the sink shelf we took from the King George hotel.'

'And?' Angel said.

And they match exactly, sir,' Taylor said.

'Good,' he said and he pointed to the chair opposite.

Taylor sat down. 'I thought you'd be pleased, sir,' he said.

'Well, yes Don, but I expected it. It further strengthens our theory that the murders were committed by the same person. It's a pity we can't find the actual glasses and bottle.'

'Probably never will, sir. After all, there are millions of glasses and bottles out there in pubs, clubs, hotels, bars, as well as in domestic situations.'

'True, but nevertheless we are making progress, Don. We know the murderer is a woman and that she almost certainly committed both murders. We also know how they were committed, and have identified the poison. What we don't know is the motive.'

'You've got nowhere with that, sir?'

Angel wrinkled his nose. 'No.'

'About the fruit gums, sir.'

'What about them?'

'I was thinking, perhaps the fruit gums have nothing to do with the two murders.'

Angel frowned. 'What do you mean?'

'Well, perhaps it's just a coincidence that there was one at each scene.'

The muscles round Angel's mouth tightened. 'A coincidence?' he said. 'Two men murdered by the same poison in hotel bedrooms in the same town in the same way in the same week and a solitary fruit gum of the same make in the same colour is found near each body, and you *think* it might be a . . . a coincidence?'

Taylor shuffled in the chair uneasily. 'Ah, well, I didn't quite mean it like that, sir. I meant, are we not putting too much emphasis on the fact that they were there? I mean, what were they there for? Why were they there? What do they represent?'

'I don't know,' Angel said, 'unless it was the intention to push the blame onto Johnson. He was found to be eating them and he had a bagful in his pocket when he was brought in. If it was, she was wasting her time.'

Taylor was overwhelmed by Angel's positive attitude so strongly put. 'It was just a thought, sir.'

'That's all right, Don. Now push off and let me get some work done.'

'Right, sir,' he said and went smartly out of the office and closed the door.

Angel watched him go and the door close, then he looked up at the clock. It was 9.00 a.m. He tossed the pamphlet back onto the pile, picked up the phone, found Crisp's number and clicked it in.

It was soon answered.

'Now then, lad,' Angel said. 'What have you got?'

'Good morning, sir,' Crisp said. 'Nothing very illuminating. I went straight to the house and found that it was a big, old, detached house owned by a woman, Mrs Rimmington-Jones, aged about sixty, who had had the house divided into several flats. She let one out to Patrick Novak, and he had lived there on his own for more than twelve years. She wasn't much bothered about his death. All she was worried about was how soon his stuff could be moved out to allow a new tenant in. She said that he was two months behind with his rent and that she was getting fed up with him. She knew he was away and she had expected him back on Saturday or Sunday. He had told her that he had gone to collect a debt and that he expected to bring his rent up to date when he got back.'

'Did you get into his flat?'

'Yes. It was a bit tatty. I had a good look round, but I didn't find anything that you might call incriminating.'

'Did you find any photographs?'

He hesitated then said, 'No, sir. I don't think so.'

Angel squeezed the phone tightly and bellowed, 'What do you mean, "I don't *think* so"?'

'I mean . . . as far as I can remember . . .'

'It was only last night, for goodness' sake!' he roared. Then he said, 'Did you find a camera?'

'Oh yes, sir. Several . . . old ones . . . *and* a tripod.'

'But no photographs. Didn't you find that odd?'

He hesitated. 'Erm . . . well, now that I come to think about it . . .'

'I'm coming down,' Angel said. 'Book me a room for tonight.'

The train slowly pulled into platform one, Norwich railway station, at 3.45 p.m. Angel was standing at the open window of a door, as it glided past the few people on the platform. When the train stopped, Angel opened the door and came down the step onto the platform, carrying a valise.

Crisp appeared from nowhere and came rushing up to him. 'There you are, sir.' He reached out for the valise. 'I'll take that, sir.'

Angel gently resisted him. 'No. That's all right, lad. Thank you. Where's the car?'

'At the front, sir. Not far. Just through the barrier and round the corner.'

When they were settled in the car, Crisp said, 'Where do you want to go first, sir?'

'Take me to Novak's flat. I suppose we can get into it?'

'Oh yes,' Crisp said and he let in the clutch. 'I've got a key, so we needn't disturb Mrs Rimmington-Jones.'

'I'd like to see her anyway. She seems to know more about Patrick Novak than anybody else.'

Crisp turned into Thorpe Road and twenty minutes later arrived at 12, Lilac Avenue, Coalsden.

It was a huge house set in a vast garden. The house had grey stucco walls, cracked and falling away in places. The windows were small and from the outside looked dark. The entire garden needed weeding, the lawns required cutting, the roses should have been dead-headed, many plants needed pruning and splitting, and the paths and driveway were in need of plentiful applications of weedkiller.

Crisp stopped the car at the side door and let himself in. Angel followed and the two men made their way up the narrow stairs to a long corridor of many doors. At one of the doors, they stopped. Crisp inserted a key in the lock. The door opened onto a small room with a table, bed, television set, several chairs and a chest of drawers. There was a door in the wall opposite, which was open, and a small window with the sun streaming through facing the garden. Angel looked through the door and saw a sink, a gas oven, a fridge, a small worktop area and another door. This led to a compact bathroom and toilet.

Angel turned back and went straight to the chest of drawers. The top drawer contained clean shirts, underclothes, socks and so on. The middle drawer was full of dusty and scratched photographic tackle. There was a Leica camera and a Baldini, an enlarger, two light meters, flash bulbs, a tripod, developing and fixing dishes and two unopened packs of roll film dated up to July 2001. There was also a roller for producing glossy prints and a small guillotine for trimming them. Angel closed that drawer and opened the bottom one, which contained boots, old shoes and slippers. He quickly closed the drawer and turned to Crisp.

'Is this all there is, Trevor?'

'Yes, sir. There's a suit of clothes and a raincoat hanging on a coat hanger on the back of the door.'

Angel went into the bathroom. It was dark. There was no window allowing natural light. He fumbled around the doorway, looking for the light switch.

Crisp saw him. 'It's a pull-switch just inside, sir,' he said.

Angel found it, pulled it, then turned back to him and said, 'Thank you. Did you come across a red electric lamp when you were searching the place?'

'A red electric lamp? There's one resting on a dusty dry flannel on top of the bathroom cupboard, sir. I think you can just see it.'

'Ah, yes,' Angel said. He reached up, took down the lamp, looked at it, replaced it, found that his fingers were covered in dust and hairs, ran his hand under the sink tap and wiped it on a towel. Then he opened the bathroom cupboard door, glanced inside and closed it.

He came out of the bathroom, looked across at Crisp and said, 'So . . . Patrick Novak had been a keen photographer . . . he took photographs, developed them, enlarged them, trimmed them . . . and then hid them.'

Crisp looked at him and frowned.

Angel rubbed his chin and said, 'But where?'

'And why?' Crisp said.

'I daresay we'll know the why when we know the where.'

There was an unexpected knock on the door.

Angel frowned and looked at Crisp, who shrugged. Angel waved a hand towards the door and Crisp stepped forward. Before he could reach the handle, the door opened and a woman looked in.

When she saw him, she smiled and said, 'Oh, Mr Crisp. I thought I heard voices.' Then she looked at Angel.

Crisp smiled, then he said, 'Mrs Rimmington-Jones, this is my boss, Detective Inspector Angel.'

She looked surprised. 'Oh. I didn't know,' she said. 'Is everything all right?'

'Pleased to meet you, Mrs Rimmington-Jones,' Angel said. 'I'm on a flying visit to support my colleague, DS Crisp. There are a few matters you might be able to help us with. And I'd like to ask you a few questions.'

She looked Angel up and down. A smile slowly developed across her normally tight and downturned lips. 'With pleasure, Inspector. How can I help?' she said.

Angel smiled and nodded. 'In particular, I need to find out Patrick Novak's next of kin.'

'I can't help you there, Inspector,' she said. 'Mr Novak had been a tenant of mine for twelve years and in all that time I never heard him speak about any relative, nor did he correspond — as far as I know — with any. I took in his post when he was at work.'

Angel frowned. 'I understand that he was a bit of a photographer?'

'I believe so. In his early days here, he frequently got parcels and correspondence from firms that supply photographers. But not so much lately.'

'What did he photograph?'

'Do you know, Inspector Angel, I don't think I ever saw anything he photographed.'

'DS Crisp will have told you that we are from Bromersley police force because he died on our patch. Can you tell me what he was doing in Bromersley?'

'I have never known him make such a trip. It was unusual for him. He owed me three months' rent. That's all I know. He said that he'd soon be able to pay it back, but he had to be away for a few days to settle up a bit of business.'

Angel rubbed a hand across his cheek and jaw. 'But he didn't say with whom?'

'No. I'm afraid not.'

'Do you know where he banked?'

'I don't think he used a bank. He once told me he couldn't trust them. Whenever he paid the rent, it was always in cash.'

'Did he have a mobile phone?'

'I never saw him with one. He seemed to favour the public phone box on Coalsden Road.'

'Was he in regular employment?'

'Well, Inspector, there's an unusual thing. He was a porter at Coalsden Cottage Hospital. He had been there for years, then one day it seemed he left and retired . . . last year, October time. I personally didn't think he was old enough to be drawing his old-age pension. I thought he was only in his fifties. But ever since then, I've had difficulty getting him to pay his rent on time.'

'Didn't he try to get another job?'

'I've no idea. I suppose so. He didn't confide in me, Inspector. He didn't confide in anyone, as far as I know.' She shook her head. 'He was an odd man,' she added.

'Where's this cottage hospital, Mrs Rimmington-Jones?'

'It's only two miles away, just off the Norwich Road. At the end of Duck Lane.'

TWELVE

After passing two farms and a duck pond, and driving though a ford, a high stone wall with large, black-painted iron gates in the open position came into view. On one of the gates was a signpost.

Angel saw it coming and said, 'Slow down, Trevor, and let's read what it says.'

Crisp put his foot on the brake.

The sign read: 'Private. Coalsden Cottage Hospital. Patients may be visited by prior arrangement only. Quiet aids recovery. Use of car horns prohibited. Maximum speed 10 mph. Please use designated car parks. All enquiries to Marjorie Underbank, Bursar.'

'Right,' Angel said. 'This must be it.'

Crisp shoved the gear stick into first and let in the clutch. As they went through the gates, they found themselves on a long drive up to a large Georgian building resembling a stately home.

'Looks a bit grand for a cottage hospital,' Angel said. 'Drive up to the entrance, Trevor. Drop me off, park up and join me.'

'Right, sir.'

Angel made his way to reception. He showed his ID to a young woman and said, 'I want to see Miss Marjorie Underbank, the bursar, urgently, please.'

'Certainly,' she said. 'I'll see if she's in.'

He waited five minutes and a woman came out to him. He saw from a badge pinned to her jacket that her name was Trudi Templeton, and that she was the assistant bursar. 'We don't often have a visit from the police,' she said. 'What can I do for you, Inspector?'

'Miss Templeton, I understand that you had an employee, Patrick Novak, working here as a porter?'

Her face changed. The corners of her mouth turned downwards and her eyelids lowered. 'Oh, I see. For all inquiries about employees, Inspector, you will need our HR department.'

Angel said, 'Well, would you kindly direct me to the person in charge of the HR department, then?'

'Certainly. It's down this corridor and the first door on the left.'

'Thank you,' he said and set off determinedly along the corridor. He found the entrance to the HR office. It was a big white door with a glass panel in it.

He tried the door and discovered it was locked. He was surprised. There was some small writing painted in the corner of the pane of glass, which read: 'Human Resources office. Open Monday to Thursday 9 a.m. to 5 p.m.; Friday 9 a.m. to 4.30 p.m. Closed Saturday and Sunday.'

He looked at his watch. It said ten to five. He clenched his fists, breathed out heavily and returned to the reception desk.

'Your Miss Templeton said that I needed to see the director of your HR department. I have just been down there and the office is closed.'

'Ah yes, sir. Well, you see, it is Friday and the HR office closes at 4.30 on a—'

The muscles on Angel's face tightened. 'I know that now, miss,' he said. 'Can I see Miss Marjorie Underbank urgently? She is the bursar, isn't she?'

'Oh yes, sir. I'll see if she's in. Please take a seat.'

He hesitated. 'Tell her the matter is urgent,' he said.

He then left the desk and sat down in the end one of a row of chairs along the wall of the entrance hall.

Crisp came into the hall. He looked around, saw Angel and sat in the seat next to his. 'Have you seen her, sir?'

Angel looked at him, his lips taut, and said, 'I haven't seen anybody helpful up to now.'

A few minutes later, Trudi Templeton appeared. She looked troubled. She came across to them.

Angel and Crisp stood up. She looked at Crisp and then at Angel.

'He is with me,' Angel said. 'This is my sergeant, DS Crisp.'

She nodded quickly, then said, 'Ah. All the hospital administration offices will be closing in the next few minutes, gentlemen. We finish at five o'clock. And, as it's Friday, you will have to come back when we reopen on Monday morning.'

Angel ran his hand through his hair, drew in a big breath and said, 'I cannot possibly wait until Monday morning, Miss Templeton. I have travelled a hundred miles as quickly as I could from a crime scene to make inquiries into the murder of one of your ex-employees.'

'Murder?' she said. Her hands went to her face. 'Patrick Novak?'

'It is extremely important that I get some information about him now,' Angel said. 'Monday morning may well be too late. The murderer has the opportunity to commit a dozen or more murders in that time. If I don't get some serious attention to my inquiries instantly, I will subpoena the entire management of this hospital, prosecute any recalcitrant for obstructing the police in the execution of their duty, and get a court order to close this hospital down and have all the patients transferred.'

'Oh. Oh!' Trudi Templeton said, and she ran off towards her office, then she stopped, came back and breathlessly said, 'Excuse me, gentlemen. I won't be a minute.'

Angel nodded. 'Thank you. We will wait here.'

She raced off.

Crisp looked from her to Angel and said, 'You can't really do all that, sir, can you?'

'No,' Angel said. 'But *she* doesn't know that, and we have to move on quickly with our inquiries. From the moment a crime has been committed, evidence is being contaminated, some intentionally, some through ignorance and some through natural progression. The only way we can counter the situation is by moving rapidly ourselves. But you know all about that. That's the sort of elementary stuff they taught you at Hendon.'

Crisp said, 'Yes, sir. It's a pity we can't freeze the scene of crime and the relationship between the victim and the villain to the moment just before the murder is committed. That would make detection a lot easier.'

'That's a bit fanciful, I think, Trevor. If we could extend that moment even more, maybe we'd be able to stop the crime being committed in the first place?'

It was at that moment that Trudi Templeton rushed back up to them and said, 'Ah, Inspector, Mrs Underbank would like to see you. Will you follow me?'

'Thank you,' Angel said, and the two men stood up and followed her.

They were shown into a comfortable-looking room with a large desk and several chairs in front of it. Sitting behind the desk was a portly, middle-aged woman with a face like thunder. She was holding a pair of spectacles.

As they came in, she stood up, looked at them, nodded and held out her hand, 'Good afternoon, Inspector, please sit down.' They shook hands. 'And you must be the sergeant. Good afternoon. Please sit down.'

'Thank you,' Angel said.

'I'm sorry that we didn't get off to a very good start, Inspector. The truth is partly because we are somewhat embarrassed that Patrick Novak was ever employed here. But Trudi tells me that he has been murdered?'

'That's right, Mrs Underbank. And I have the unenviable task of finding out who murdered him. There are some questions I would like to ask about him.'

At that point, Angel took a miniaturized tape recorder out of his pocket and said, 'Have you any objection to recording our conversation? It will avoid taking notes and save time.'

She shook her head and made a gesture to place the machine wherever he wanted on her desk.

'Thank you,' Angel said. 'Now, Mrs Underbank, Patrick Novak worked here for some years, didn't he?'

'Must have been around fifteen years, Inspector. I was the one who interviewed him and recommended his appointment as a porter/handyman to the board. That was one of my bad decisions. But he was very good at his job. Reliable. Good timekeeper. Although most of his time was spent wheeling patients round the hospital, he was very handy at small electrical and carpentry jobs, and painting and decorating. We never had any complaints about him. Some patients even told us what little services and shopping he'd done for them. We only had good reports about him. That was until last October.'

'Well, please tell me, what happened last October?'

'Before I go there, Inspector, let me say something about this hospital. Coalsden Hospital is a private hospital, and private surgery and nursing is expensive. It is specialized and labour-intensive, so we tend to get moneyed patients, including some minor royalty, titled and business people, politicians and pop stars. And people both in the public eye and out of the public eye would rather have their hernias and haemorrhoids confidentially treated here than have every surgical procedure and operation reported in detail in the newspapers. Some come here to have their unwanted babies, which is very sad. They also come here for cosmetic surgery. So you can understand that confidentiality is very important.'

Angel nodded. 'Yes, indeed, but please tell me about last October.'

'Of course,' she said. 'I received an anonymous letter saying that Patrick Novak had been selling to newspapers photographs of patients which had obviously been taken without their knowledge. We knew that some of this had been happening, but we had no idea of the culprit. We thought it must have been a visitor. Anyway, I had Novak in here and confronted him with it. He didn't deny it. He boasted that it was him and that he had being doing it for some time. I had no choice but to dismiss him. He responded by rattling off a list of long-standing grievances he had against me in particular and the hospital in general and stormed out. And that, I thought, was the end of it.'

'Until today,' Angel said. He briefly explained the circumstances of Novak's death, then took out the small photograph he had found in the man's wallet and passed it to her.

'Was this photograph taken in this hospital?'

She put on her glasses and peered closely at it. 'Well, Inspector, possibly. The truth is it could have been taken in just about any hospital . . . anywhere.'

'Is the date on the back of the photograph significant?'

She turned the photograph over. 'May 2nd, 2002,' she said. 'Means nothing to me.'

She pushed the photograph back along the desk towards him.

'I am assuming it is the date the photograph was taken. Do your records go back as far as 2002?'

'Well, some do. I'm not sure all the medical records will, but certainly the accounts do, all the way back to when I came in 1999. The information is all on two memory sticks.'

'So you would know who was a patient in the hospital on that date?'

She frowned and pulled off her glasses. 'Not quite, Inspector,' she said. 'But we do have a record of every person, insurance company, institution or organization that actually paid a bill for treatment, since 1999. Also we have a copy of every hospital invoice. In some cases, the payee did not have the same name as the patient. However, against each payee is an invoice number that can be cross-referenced to a copy which gives the patient's name, ward number, surgeon and other details.'

Angel leaned back in the chair and smiled.

'Are you looking for any particular name, Inspector?' she said.

He shook his head. 'I wish I had a name. I am looking for a person who held a grudge against Patrick Novak and another man, Norman Robinson, so much so that they poisoned them with a ghastly home-made poison. Someone who also, for some inexplicable reason, left a fruit gum by each body.'

Mrs Underbank frowned. 'A fruit gum, Inspector?' she said.

'Peculiar, isn't it?'

She nodded and exchanged glances with Trudi Templeton.

'We are hoping that the photograph in Novak's possession,' Angel said, 'has some direct bearing on this murder and that a familiar name will be forthcoming. I believe it is somebody local to us in Bromersley, probably somebody we know and perhaps have even interviewed in the last few days.'

A mobile phone rang out. It was Angel's. He pulled a face. He stood up. 'Sorry about this,' he said. He pulled the phone out of his pocket and looked at the screen. He hoped it was not Mary again, bothering him about Mrs Mackenzie and the dance at Muick Castle. It wasn't. It was much worse. It was the superintendent. Angel went into a corner of the office . . . the furthest he could get away from Mrs Underbank and Trudi Templeton. He pressed the button and said, 'Yes, sir. Angel here.'

'Where the hell are you?' Harker said.

'Norfolk, sir. On this Novak case. I'm with a witness. Can I ring you back?'

'Norfolk? Five o'clock on a Friday afternoon and you're messing about in Norfolk? It's ridiculous. No, you can't ring me back. And you'll have to come back here double-quick,

Angel. I've just had a triple nine about a serious fire — possibly arson — at a greengrocer's shop on the corner of Station Road and Main Street.'

'Truelove's, sir?'

'That's the one. There was a dead body on the premises, a man, possibly an intruder.'

The corners of Angel's mouth turned downwards.

'Could be murder,' Harker said. 'You should be there. I've a dinner tonight in Leeds with the committee of the northern police billiards team. I've to get home and get ready for it, and I'm late now!'

Angel's heart began to pump harder. 'I'll catch the next train, sir.'

'Right. I'm leaving that with you, then.'

Harker ended the call.

Angel turned round. He ran his hand through his hair.

Mrs Underbank, Trudi Templeton and Crisp looked at him.

'Sorry about that,' he said. 'I've been ordered back.' Then he tapped a number in his mobile. 'Excuse me. I must just see to this.'

Ahmed soon answered. 'Yes, sir?'

'Ah. I know it's five past five, Ahmed, but will you see if you can catch Flora Carter for me and get her to ring me on my mobile? It's very urgent.'

'Right, sir,' Ahmed said.

Angel then closed his mobile and turned back to Mrs Underbank. 'Sorry about all this, but it's another possible murder. Can my sergeant here look through those records we were talking about? He knows what to do, don't you Trevor?'

Crisp said, 'Oh yes, sir. Record and follow through any familiar name.'

Mrs Underbank said: 'He can make copies of the two memory sticks provided that I can have his and your assurance that the information contained is only to be used in connection with the finding of the murderer of Patrick Novak.'

'Certainly,' Angel said. He turned to Crisp and said, 'We can honestly give that undertaking to Mrs Underbank, can't we, Trevor?'

'Absolutely,' Crisp said.

'Take me straight back to Norwich railway station,' Angel said as soon as he had closed the car door.

Crisp started the engine and the car glided down the hospital drive.

As the car passed through the big iron gates, Angel's mobile rang out. He dived into his pocket and opened the phone. It was DS Carter.

He explained that he was in Norfolk and that the superintendent had advised him about a fire at Truelove's greengrocer's shop. 'I want you to go there and take charge of the investigation,' he said. 'Advise Don Taylor and get a SOCO team on site. You know what to do. Ring me if you're stuck with anything. I'm coming back by the next train.'

Angel closed his phone. He rubbed his chin. He hoped that there wasn't another murder to be investigated.

Crisp carefully drove the car through the ford on his way to the main Norwich city road.

Angel was rubbing his chin. He had returned to thinking about Novak. There was something he couldn't get out of his head. Nobody could have that much photographic kit without having the end product — photographs — somewhere round about. He made a decision.

'Take me back to Novak's place, Trevor,' Angel said.

Crisp frowned. 'Right, sir,' he said, then he took a sharp turn left. 'Changed your mind, sir?' he added as he straightened up and changed gear.

'Got to find those photographs,' Angel said.

Crisp produced the key and opened the door into Patrick Novak's flat.

'Check the floor, Trevor,' Angel said. 'I'll do the walls.'

'Right, sir,' Crisp said as he closed the door.

Angel stood in the middle of the room and gazed at the walls, systematically scanning them across and down, one after the other. He was looking for a bump, a swelling, a projection that was unnecessary or illogical. There was a print of an oriental girl in a cheap frame over the mantelpiece. He lifted it up. But there was nothing underneath. He then went into the bathroom and repeated the drill.

Crisp was leaning forward, his legs stretched, pulling and pushing carpets and rugs to allow him to check the looseness of any floorboards. Each one in the living room was as rigid as Judges' Rules.

They moved into the bathroom. The only projection was the small, mirrored cupboard over the sink. Angel reached up and removed the red lamp resting on a dusty flannel on top of the cupboard and put it in the bottom of the sink. He opened the cupboard doors to see how it was fastened to the wall and saw that it was secured by the heads of two screws. The cupboard was made of plastic and weighed only a few pounds. He discovered that if he lifted it about an inch, it would be free and could be taken away. He lifted it up and put it on top of the lavatory cistern. Behind where it had been was a cavity, and stuffed into it was a small cardboard box contrived to fit the space. His pulse raced.

'Trevor,' he said. 'There's something here.'

Crisp came up from searching the floor. 'What's that?'

Angel took out the cardboard box and was looking inside it. The box contained many photographs of various sizes, taken, apparently in the hospital, of patients asleep while in bed; others were of people walking along corridors, some of patients on trolleys, some of people in lifts. Quite a few were photographs of mothers with their babies, and several, similar to the one found in Novak's wallet, were of a baby in an incubator. Not one of them appeared to have been deliberately posed for, and none of the people photographed appeared to have been aware what was happening. On the back of each was a date lightly printed in pencil.

As Angel gazed at them and turned them over, Crisp looked at them.

'Blackmail, sir?' Crisp said.

'Looks like it,' Angel said. 'So if Novak was a blackmailer . . . he must have been blackmailing somebody on our turf.'

Angel began pushing the photographs into the cardboard box. 'I'll take these with me.'

'Novak pushed too hard or asked for too much so the person being blackmailed murdered him. Do you think that's what happened, sir?'

'Probably,' he said, closing up the box. 'But was Norman Robinson also a blackmailer? We've established that both murders were carried out by the same person.'

Crisp frowned. 'That must have been for some other motive?'

'I expect so. But you have to take the whole scenario into account. For example, even if Novak was murdered because of his blackmailing activities, why was there a fruit gum by each of the dead bodies? The answer to that will likely reveal an explanation that will lead us to the murderer.'

Crisp's mouth dropped open. Then he frowned.

Angel said: 'Anyway, by the time you've got copies of those computer memory sticks from the hospital, cancelled the accommodation you had booked for me for tonight and tidied everything up here, you should be able to come home tomorrow.'

'Yes, sir,' Crisp said.

'Right, lad, now you can take me to Norwich station. I must look into that dreadful fire at old Mr Truelove's.'

THIRTEEN

It was 10 p.m. when the local train from Sheffield pulled into Bromersley station. Angel got out with the cardboard box under his arm and, carrying his valise, he walked swiftly through the ticket barrier into Station Road and then turned left towards Main Street. The smell of burning wood pervaded the air and reminded him, as if he needed reminding, of the fire at Truelove's on the corner earlier that day, which had been reported to him.

As he reached the junction he saw a fire engine and a police car, both with blue lights flashing. Behind them was the black shell of a building with several partly burned beams of the upper floors hanging down across the floors below. Around the windows, the grey stone was as black as fingerprint ink, and there was no indication that a greengrocer's had ever existed there. He now became aware of the smell of petrol.

A lone fireman was stamping around what had been the sales area of Truelove's shop, checking to see that the fire really was out. Another fireman was on the pavement, draining a canvas water-pipe and rolling it up.

In the street light, he saw that the police car was a Bromersley patrol car and that there were two uniformed men in the front seat, talking. He recognized them as PC Sean Donohue and PC Cyril Elders. Neither of them saw him approach the nearside front window, which was lowered.

He bent down and said, 'Excuse me, lads, are you dealing with anything urgent?'

They peered back through the window at Angel illuminated only by the halogen street light and intermittently by their rotating blue lamp. They eventually recognized him and were taken aback that an inspector had suddenly appeared.

Sean Donohue quickly reached out for his hat that was on top of the dashboard and put it on.

When they found their tongues, they said, 'No, sir. No, sir.'

'What can you tell me about this fire, then?'

They looked blankly at each other.

'I've been in Norwich all day,' Angel said.

Sean Donohue said, 'Oh, I see. Sorry, sir. We didn't know . . . Er, yes. This fire was notified this morning at about 9.00 a.m., by the owner, a Mr Enoch Truelove.'

'Is *he* all right, Sean?'

'No, sir. He stupidly went in, presumably to see if he could do anything. Nobody knew this. We think he was overcome by smoke because his body was later found and taken to the mortuary.'

Angel felt as if he had been kicked in the stomach by a horse.

'The fire officer says it was a petrol fire, sir, poured through the letterbox sometime in the night.'

It was ten o'clock on Saturday morning, 8th June.

Angel was walking down the corridor to his office and he peered into the CID room as he passed the door. It was deserted.

He reached his office, picked up the phone and tapped in a number.

A familiar voice said, 'Yes, sir. Control Room, Sergeant Clifton.'

Angel knew him well. 'Ah, Bernie. I was away yesterday. Anything happened?'

'Oh. Yes, sir. Nasty fire on Station Road. One man killed.'

'Yes. Dreadful. Who's dealing with it?'

'John Weightman, sir. PC Weightman. I think he's around somewhere. Saw him a few minutes ago. If you want to see him, I'll call him up on the RT. Do you want to see him?'

'Yes please, Bernie. ASAP in my office. Anything else?'

'A couple of housebreaking jobs and a domestic disturbance on Canal Street, sir. And that's it. Oh, no, we got an anonymous phone call reporting that Harry "the hatchet" Harrison and Mickey "the loop" Zeiss were reported seen coming out of the King George hotel with a girl. It was traced to that phone box opposite. A car was sent down, but if they were there they'd disappeared by the time our lads got there.'

Angel frowned then said, 'That's the second time in a fortnight we've had that report on Harrison seen at the George with a girl. Anything else?'

'No, sir. Otherwise a quiet day on the whole.'

'Who was sent down to the George?'

'Erm . . . Sean Donohue and Cyril Elders, sir.'

'I spoke to them last night around ten. They'll be off-duty now.'

'No, sir. They're doing a double shift. Summer holidays and all that. If you want to see them, I can call them in.'

'Right, Bernie, do that. I'll be in here in my office.'

There was a knock at the door and a face appeared. It was PC Weightman.

'Got a message you wanted me, sir.'

'Come in, John. Sit down. I want to ask you about yesterday's fire. I understand that you were the continuity officer.'

'Yes, that's right, sir.'

'I was away, you know. Tell me all about it. Leave nothing out. Where were you when you got the call, and who called you?'

'I was in the locker room, sir. It was about nine o'clock. I got a call from Inspector Asquith via the Operations Room to attend a triple-nine call to a fire at Truelove's on Station Road. I took the station car and went straight to it. There were flames coming through the windows and the door. And there was the unmistakable smell of petrol. There was a small group of onlookers and one came up to me and said that she had seen a man inside. He'd apparently gone in, left the door open, presumably intending to come out again, but she said he was still in there. But now you couldn't get near. There were three tenders there. I found the fire chief and told him what the woman had told me about a man being in there. He said it would be suicide for them to go in at that stage. But they'd go in as soon as they could, which they did. SOCO duly arrived with DS Taylor, and later the mortuary van. They eventually brought the body of the man somebody had identified as Enoch Truelove. It was wrapped up in an oilcloth on a stretcher and taken away in the mortuary van. By about two o'clock, they had it well under control. One of the tenders left. Inspector Asquith sent me a relief, but I didn't leave. I sat in the car and had my sandwiches and a drink. Nothing much happened for the next six hours or so. The flames were out, but the fire tenders kept pumping water into the building to cool it down. It was burning hot, even on the pavement. I had another word with the fire officer. He said that he thought that the fire was caused by the deliberate exposure of petrol fumes. The signs were that an excessive amount of petrol had been poured into the front of the shop, probably through the letterbox. He did not know what ignited it. It could have been done simply with a match, but the friction of two metal objects together, even horses' hooves on cobblestones, would have been sufficient to ignite such an inflammable atmosphere. Anyway, he left at about six o'clock, so did the second tender and SOCO. Then a patrol car team came to relieve me. I reported in at the station and signed out at about 6.20 p.m. I've had a quick look in there this morning. The lads reported a quiet night. The building is still warm but it looks a horrible mess. I expect it will have to be demolished. The woman who rented the shop upstairs as a fancy-dress hire shop was there. She said even her diary and bookings and everything has gone up in smoke. She didn't know where she was. And that's about it.'

Angel nodded. 'Thank you, John. Do you know of any motive for the fire? Was anything stolen?'

'Nothing to steal as far as we know, sir. A sack of Maris Piper would be the most valuable thing there.'

Angel shook his head.

'If there's anything else, sir?' Weightman said.

'No, lad. You get off.'

'Right, sir,' Weightman said.

'Come in,' Angel called.

It was Patrolman PC Sean Donohue. He was still in uniform, carrying his hat. 'You wanted to see me and Cyril Elders, sir? Sergeant Clifton caught me but Cyril had already gone. Did you want to see us about last night, sir?'

'No. Sit down, lad. I want to ask you about the call-out you had yesterday to the George hotel.'

Donohue blew out a cheek full of air, and sat down.

Angel sensed that he was relieved. He looked as if he had expected being disciplined for something.

'Oh, that, sir? Well, we were on patrol on Park Road and got an urgent shout from Control to respond to an anonymous call that Harry "the hatchet" Harrison and a little man, thought to be Mickey "the loop" Zeiss, had been seen coming out of the King George hotel with a girl.'

'You were in a marked car?'

'Yes, sir. Our patrol car. So we made haste down to Main Street. At the roundabout we slowed down, and made our way slowly along Main Street to the George. Didn't see anything conspicuous . . . stopped outside the front . . . I went inside the pub, looked round the bar, everything was quiet. The landlord, Jack Vermont, asked me what was wrong. I told him. He didn't seem to know anything.'

'Do you mean he denied it?'

'No, sir. He didn't deny it. He just didn't seem to know who Harrison or Mickey were.'

'What about the girl? Did you ask him about the girl?'

'Yes, but he said he hadn't noticed anything.'

'Was the pub busy?'

'Not particularly. There'd be about a dozen men in there.'

'Any women?'

'I don't think so.'

Angel rubbed his chin. 'And did you believe him?'

'Don't know, sir. I had to act on what he said.'

'If there'd been two men and a girl in a pub with another twelve men, would you have noticed the girl?'

Donohue hesitated. 'Probably, sir.'

Angel's jaw muscles tightened. 'I'm damned certain you would, lad.' He rubbed his chin harder. 'Do you know what Harrison and Mickey look like?'

'I saw them on a handout on parade about three months ago.'

'Could you describe either of them to me?'

Donohue frowned. 'Erm, well, they are rather ordinary, sir.'

'Aye, well that's true. Neither wears an eyepatch, has a parrot on his shoulder or walks with a crutch.'

It was one o'clock.

Angel put the ever-growing pile of papers into a drawer, glanced round the little office, then closed the door. He was going home. He had finished all the jobs he had set himself to do, and he was determined to make the most of the rest of the weekend. He had promised Mary he would cut the lawn, and the borders at the front of the house needed weeding.

On the way home it clouded over and started to rain. He wasn't too disappointed. He put the BMW in the garage, locked it and let himself into the house. Unusually, Mary was nowhere to be seen. He went to the fridge and took out a can of German beer. Then he thought he could hear her banging around upstairs. He went to the bottom of the stairs and looked upwards.

'Mary,' he called. 'Light of my life. Mary, where are you? My little cuddle bunch.'

She was in the bedroom. She smiled. She knew why he was calling her like that. He wanted some lunch.

'I'm coming,' she called. 'Have you been drinking?'

He smiled. 'If you mean alcohol, darling, no. If you mean drinking in your beauty . . . well, that's a very different matter.'

Mary smiled, shook her head and quickly prepared a snack lunch of tomato soup with brown bread followed by two sweet and juicy Conference pears.

They ate without talking until Angel, apropos of nothing at all, said, 'You know, old man Truelove must have known something that worried the murderer.'

'What do you mean, darling?' Mary said. She finished peeling a pear and added, 'He's hardly likely to have gone into his shop and said, "I'll take those flowers. These are for my friend Charlie Smith. He is going to poison me." Would he?'

'You've forgotten, sweetheart, that we now think the murderer is a woman.'

'All right. "These are for my friend Agnes Smith. She is going to poison me." '

'No. No. He wouldn't know she intended poisoning him, would he?'

'No. Of course not. Well, she may have seen Trevor Crisp or you visiting him, and knowing you were the police . . .'

Angel's face straightened. 'I should hate to think I was in any way the cause of his death,' he said.

'I don't suppose you were for one moment, love. But you can't tell how people will react. And it's only conjecture anyway.'

'You can't. You're right,' he said and helped himself to another pear. He pulled out the stem and began to peel it. 'It was a terrible fire,' he said.

'Yes. I understand that it was so intense, it burned everything in Mr Truelove's shop as well as everything in the fancy-dress hire shop above it?'

'Nothing left in either shop. All her stock went up in flames. I hope the poor woman was insured.'

'Yes, love. I expect she was . . . well, that actually leaves us in a bit of a mess.'

He frowned. 'Eh?'

'I had hired a fez, a cummerbund and a big curly moustache for you from her for next Saturday's Fancy-Dress Ball. In your new dark suit, I had a great vision of you being somebody Turkish. You would have looked fantastic as "the Turkish Ambassador".'

Angel's eyes shone like a cat's in the dark. 'Oh my goodness! I would have looked a right Charlie!'

She laughed.

He put another piece of pear in his mouth. 'What were you going as? The Turkish Ambassador's wife?'

'I was going as a slave girl.'

He smiled. 'You might be the prettiest female there, sweetheart, but you're a bit old to be a slave girl.'

'Steady on, Father Time,' she said. 'The thing is . . . what are we going to do about our fancy dress now?'

The weekend came and went, and Angel still hadn't cut the lawn because of the rain. It never seemed to stop.

It was 8.28 a.m., Monday morning, 10th June. Angel was in his office trying to decide on his priorities. There was so much to do.

There was a knock at the door.

It was DS Crisp. 'Good morning, sir.'

'There you are, lad. Did you have a good journey?'

'Yes, sir. I got everything done there and I came home on Saturday afternoon.'

'You got those memory sticks?'

'Yes, sir,' he said. He put the two penknife-shaped objects on the desk. 'It will be a daunting job checking that lot off.'

Angel picked them up and looked at them. 'Often that's what police work is all about,' he said. 'Here you are,' he added, passing them back to him. 'Go through them. You know what we are looking for: a name, a familiar name out of all the people we've interviewed or seen or heard of, who might have held a grudge against Patrick Novak and Norman Robinson.'

Crisp wasn't pleased. 'That'll take ages.'

'It's a long shot,' Angel said. 'But it's the only shot left to us.'

'Right, sir,' he said, and went out.

Angel wondered if he had done the right thing in allocating that job to Crisp. It was a job that might have been better undertaken by Ahmed, who was most careful and systematic. However, Ahmed had a lot on at that time. Crisp was better employed persuading pretty female witnesses to confide in him, or tackling a tricky male suspect who tried to flex his muscles rather than answer awkward questions. He shrugged. All was not lost. It could always be changed.

He pulled the pile of papers with the ever-present ugly ornament on the top.

There was a knock at the door.

'Come in,' he called.

It was Flora Carter. Her face was red and her eyes were bright.

Angel knew she had something important on her mind. 'Yes,' he said, pointing to the other chair. 'What's up?'

She sat down. She waved her mobile phone at him and said, 'I just overheard a conversation between Harrison and Thomas Johnson. His mobile only seems to be used to communicate between the two of them. And Harrison is very guarded in what he says. He doesn't use people's names, or places. Only letters.'

'Like a sort of code or shorthand?'

'Yes,' she said. 'He had a conversation with him a couple of minutes ago. I came straight to you. It seems to me that he wants a certain C to meet him at the G at two o'clock today. Now, sir, I interpret that to mean that he wants a girl called Christine or Carol, or some other girl whose Christian name begins with C, to meet him at two o'clock at the King George hotel.'

Angel frowned. 'Could be. That C could be that young girl he keeps being seen with. Why do you think he is telling Johnson?'

'Presumably because Johnson knows the C girl, and can arrange it.'

Angel rubbed his chin. 'He's already been seen twice in the vicinity of the King George, with a young girl. Don't you think he'd have more sense and change his meeting place?'

'You would think so, sir,' Flora said. 'It's only an educated guess on my part, of course. The G could also stand for the gym. There's that gym on that little street off Canal Road.'

Angel didn't reply for a few moments, then he said, 'Harrison trusts Thomas Johnson, doesn't he, Flora?'

'He seems to, sir. Yes.'

'Well, what would he do if he thought Johnson had given him away to the police, for instance?'

Her eyes flashed. 'Who knows? He wouldn't be pleased.'

'Right. Let's give him something to be displeased about. At the same time, we can check to see whether your interpretation of their code or shorthand is right or not. Hmm. Two o'clock today, you said?'

FOURTEEN

It was 1.45 p.m. that Monday, when Angel went into Ives the Chemists on Main Street in the centre of Bromersley. He was met by Mr Ives Senior and was immediately shown upstairs into their first-floor storeroom. It had a window through which Angel could see the front entrance of the King George hotel. Angel thanked Mr Ives and then the elderly man went back downstairs.

At 1.50 p.m., two marked police patrol cars, Red Tango 1 and Red Tango 2, took up their designated positions. Each car had a driver and a co-driver who had in his possession a Heckler & Koch G36 C Rifle, which was out of sight of passers-by, but could be accessed by the patrolman in a second. Red Tango 1 drove onto a quiet corner of the big car park of the gym on Sykes Street off Canal Road, while Red Tango 2 drove round the back of the King George hotel. At 1.58 p.m., DS Flora Carter parked her car on a space at the back door of the chemists usually reserved by a car owned by Mr Ives Senior.

Angel carefully placed his Glock G17 pistol, binoculars and camera on the window ledge in the chemist's storeroom. He put on the earpiece of his RT set and called up each of the three units until they were all online.

Then he said, 'The first stage of this operation, remember, is to unsettle Harrison and Mickey. However we may not see them because they are very clever and very careful. They may come in disguise. They may not come at all. Afterwards, you may think they have not been. I ask you all to look vigilant and attentive, to keep your eyes open and not to take any action without first speaking to me. Also I ask you to report any sighting of Thomas Johnson, possibly with a female described as a girl. She'll likely be "on the game" and probably known to us. Even if you don't see any of them, it doesn't mean that this exercise has necessarily failed. They or their lookouts will have seen you, and for this first stage of the exercise, I believe the operation will have been successful. It is now 2.00 p.m. Call out if you see anything of them or anything suspicious.'

Angel took out his binoculars. He adjusted the focus, then scanned Main Street and the pavement at the other side of the road. He followed the pedestrians all the way to the entrance to the King George hotel. It was not very busy. Then he saw the burly figure of Thomas Johnson, who was taking big strides up the road. Beside him, a slim young woman with a big head of dark hair, in a short dress with no sleeves, was struggling to keep up. Angel trained the binoculars on her. He could see she was walking uncomfortably as her shoes had inordinately high heels. Presumably, she had not yet mastered how to walk elegantly in them. He couldn't detect the detail of any of her facial features, but she plainly was wearing unusually orange-coloured lipstick.

They got nearer. He picked up the camera, pointed it at the girl. He clicked it and kept clicking until she went into the hotel. Then he picked up the binoculars.

'Calling Red Tango 2,' Angel said.

'Red Tango 2,' came the reply.

'Johnson and a slim young woman with a thick head of black hair have just entered the front entrance of the King George. So keep your eyes peeled. Have you noticed anybody observing you at all?'

'Not that we know of, sir.'

'Right. Now calling Red Tango 1.'

'Red Tango 1. Nothing to report here, sir.'

'Right,' Angel said. Then, through his binoculars, he saw something that wasn't expected. A big red car pulled up outside the front entrance of the hotel, the car door opened, then out of the revolving door ran Johnson and the young woman. They began to pile into the car. Angel's pulse rate quickened. He grabbed the camera and clicked away several times as the car door closed and the car raced away.

His jaw dropped. That was unexpected.

'Calling cars Red Tango 1 and Red Tango 2,' he said. 'Leave your current positions and follow a big red car at present leaving the front of the King George hotel and travelling eastwards.'

Both Red Tango 1 and 2 acknowledged the instruction, then Angel said, 'Calling DS Carter.'

'DS Carter here, sir.'

'Come round to the front of the shop and pick me up ASAP.'

'Right, sir.'

Then Angel pocketed the Glock pistol, put his binoculars and camera round his neck and rushed down the stairs. He waved a thank you in the direction of the shop counter and hurried out onto the pavement on Main Street just as DS Carter arrived. She stopped the car at the side of him. He snatched open the front door, jumped into the car as she deftly pulled away in the direction of the villain's car.

An hour and a half later, both patrol car crews, plus DS Carter and Angel, trudged into the briefing room at Bromersley station and sat down. None of the cars had picked up the path the villains' car had taken, nor had Angel been able to spot and record the car's make and registration number.

Angel stood up and said, 'I want to thank all who took part in this operation this afternoon. Although we failed to see or arrest Harrison or Mickey "the loop" Zeiss, the operation has been far from a washout. Firstly, they still don't know that we are monitoring the telephone calls between Johnson and Harrison. Secondly, it has now been established that DS Carter has accurately worked out the simple code in those calls. For instance, we now know that the letter G stands for the George hotel and not the gym. So we are now well placed to find out what is happening between them, and hopeful of receiving information that will lead to us arresting them all and putting them away for good very soon. Thirdly, I don't think they know that we were observing them today. Fourthly, we have a pretty good idea that the landlord, Jack Vermont, must be closing a blind eye to Harrison and his gang using his pub as a meeting-house, therefore we need to give him a wide berth until we are ready to prosecute. And fifthly, we now have photographs of Harrison's girlfriend. From those pictures, I am hopeful that we might identify her.'

Several of the team nodded and muttered agreeably.

'Any questions?' Angel said.

'Yes, sir,' Flora said. 'What are we going to do about the Harrison gang now? I mean, we are not going to leave the situation like this, are we?'

'No, Sergeant. We're going to wait until you — hopefully — overhear Harrison setting up another meeting. And let's hope it is very soon.'

Then Angel said, 'Anything else?'

Patrolman Sean Donohue put up a hand.

Angel nodded and said, 'Sean?'

'Yes, sir. Why were we parked at the back of the King George? Why not at the front?'

'I thought that Harrison intended meeting Johnson and the girl inside the hotel, and I didn't want them thinking that we knew he was going to be there but that the patrol car driver — you in this instance — and his mate were having a natural break and that police presence was a coincidence. The plan was not to have them rush off like that, but to make them nervous enough not to settle there. Also I didn't think he would arrive by car. I thought he would park up somewhere and walk it to the hotel. Anyway, someone obviously saw your patrol car, probably the landlord Vermont, phoned it through to Harrison, who changed his plans at the last minute and made his escape with the girl, as we all know.'

Donohue nodded.

'Anything else?' He looked round the room. 'All right, thank you, chaps. Time is 3.20 p.m. Return to your usual duties.'

He turned to DS Carter. 'Thank you, Flora,' he said and made for the door.

On his way back to his office he passed the CID room, where he stopped, pushed the glass door open and saw Ahmed working at his desk. 'Ahmed,' he said.

The young man jumped up and said, 'Yes, sir?'

Angel gestured for him to come out into the hall.

'Come down to my office, lad. I want you to take my camera. I took ten or a dozen photographs of a young woman. We are trying to identify her. Will you reproduce the best onto the computer, enlarge them to the clearest picture and, well, you . . . you know what to do. Then print them off. Let me see the best.'

'Right, sir.'

It was nine o'clock Tuesday morning, the 11th June. Ahmed came into Angel's office. He was carrying a yellow paper file.

'I've got those photographs of the girl and the car, sir,' Ahmed said. 'I've put them through the identification website but she doesn't seem to be known. That's if it works.'

Angel took the file. 'What do you mean — if it works?'

'Well, sir, if we can rely on it to be accurate.'

Angel opened the file. 'I'm told that it is very accurate, lad. There's something individual — like fingerprints — about the eyes.'

He looked through the neat colour prints of the girl that he had prepared.

'Ah, well, maybe it needs a full-frontal shot of the face, sir,' Ahmed said. 'And you didn't get that.'

'No, lad, I didn't,' he said.

He turned over the last print and said, 'I don't recognize her. But that orange lipstick is very distinctive. I haven't seen orange-coloured lipstick since . . . well, for years. We'll have to keep looking.' He selected the best print and said, 'Create a "Wanted" poster, A4 size, for internal use only, using this photograph. Print off enough for everyone at the briefing meeting at the ten o'clock parade and a few others for the reception and the canteen noticeboards. And see to the distribution, will you?'

Ahmed nodded.

Angel said, 'If we can get that girl, we have a chance at bottling Harrison through his back door.'

Ahmed frowned. 'His back door, sir?'

'Attacking him from a direction he wouldn't expect,' he said impatiently. 'Anything else?'

'The car, sir.'

Angel said, 'Oh yes?'

'The photographs are a bit blurred, but I know a bit about it.'

Angel was surprised. He looked up at him. 'What do you know, lad?'

'Well, it's a Jaguar 3-litre V6 turbocharged diesel, sir. It has four doors, so it's in their LWB Portfolio range. It's in metallic paint which Jaguar call Italian Racing Red.'

Angel frowned. He was amazed that Ahmed knew so much about it.

He rubbed his chin. 'Are you sure?' he said.

'You can see the Kasuga alloy wheels, the twin tailpipes and the XJ badge on the left side of the boot lid, sir. Oh yes, sir, I'm sure. I'm positive.'

Angel sniffed and said, 'And I suppose you know how much it cost?'

'Oh yes, sir. Just under £71,000.'

Angel blinked. 'It's a pity we couldn't get the registration number. You'd better put it on the PNC and see if it's wanted.'

'I have already done that, sir, without the registration and there's no match.'

'You're making me feel superfluous, lad.'

Ahmed smiled. 'I might be useful gathering up the info, sir, but you're the one who puts it all together, fills in the gaps and makes sense of it all.'

Angel pulled an unhappy face and said, 'Aye. I do.' Then he breathed out deeply and added, 'Sometimes.'

'You will, sir. You will.'

'Right. Crack on with that "Wanted" poster then.'

Ahmed went out.

Angel rubbed the temples at the side of his head. He relaxed his face muscles. His eyes were tired. He closed them briefly. Then he dragged open the top drawer of the desk. He thought he might have some paracetamol tablets somewhere. He couldn't find them. He slammed it shut and pulled open another drawer and scrabbled around inside it. He closed that one and opened the bottom one.

There was a knock at the door.

'Come in,' he called, still rummaging in the drawer.

It was Flora Carter. 'Oh I'm glad you're free, sir,' she said.

Angel looked up. She was panting. Her cheeks were red and her eyes were shining like car headlights.

He closed the drawer, pointed to a chair and said, 'Whatever's the matter, lass?'

'I've just overheard a conversation between Harrison and Thomas Johnson.'

Angel looked up. He forgot the paracetamol. 'Yes? Go on,' he said.

'I wrote it down so that I shouldn't get it wrong.' She looked at her notebook and said, 'Harrison has just phoned Thomas Johnson and told him to book a suite in the F for tomorrow in the name of MacDonald. As it's a posh pad, get C to wear a smart dark suit. To go out and buy one if necessary. And he told him to smarten himself up as well and to put on a tie. To bring her in at two o'clock. And he said that he would be there before then.'

Angel rubbed his chin and smiled.

'Great stuff, Flora. Hop off and tell Trevor Crisp, Ahmed, Ted Scrivens and Leisha Baverstock that I want them in the briefing room in ten minutes.'

'Right, sir.'

He reached out for the phone and tapped in a number.

He was soon speaking to his old friend Detective Inspector Waldo White, at Wakefield, who was in charge of the Firearms Security Unit.

After some friendly banter, Angel said, 'It's like this, Waldo: we have reliable information that Harry "the hatchet" Harrison has arranged for a rendezvous with a regular tart at the Feathers hotel here in Bromersley tomorrow at two o'clock. He seems to have the hots for her. Thomas Johnson will be bringing the girl, and Mickey "the loop" Zeiss may also be there.'

White gave a short, one-note whistle. 'Wow! Hey, Michael, that would be quite a coup. Wasn't it Harrison who shot that van driver in Essex, then beheaded the poor man with a meat cleaver?'

'Yes, simply because the van driver tried to prevent him stealing his cargo of gold bars. And there are three other cases of murder executed in exactly the same way. It has become his trademark.'

'Shocking,' White said. 'And alarming,' he added.

'Well, it is very likely that Harrison and Mickey will be armed.'

'What is known about this Mickey "the loop" Zeiss? Such a daft name.'

'Aye. All I know is that he's from Austria, he's only a little man, and he does Harrison's dirty work. That is, killing to order. We can't be certain about Thomas Johnson and the girl. Now, Waldo, we cannot put any of the public who may be in any part of the hotel at risk. Nor can we ban the public from the place or take those sorts of precautions because Harrison would notice and may start firing off or take flight. Therefore we must wait until he and whoever else is present are settled and assembled in the one room, and then they must be surprised and overwhelmed before they can reach for their weapons. That's the brief.'

FIFTEEN

It was noon the next day, Wednesday, 12th June.

On the first floor of the Feathers hotel was Suite 1, which had been reserved for the 'MacDonald' party. Opposite the main door to that suite was the door to a service room, which was where early-morning teas and room service were provided. In the corner was a dumb waiter used for delivering food and drink directly from the kitchen to the room service staff. The room was also used also for storing clean linen, table napkins, cutlery, coasters, breakfast trays, small pots of jam and marmalade, spare bedside cabinets and so on.

On that Wednesday afternoon, eleven men and one woman were crammed into that little room. There were the eight men from the Firearms Security Unit comprising six PCs, a sergeant and DI Waldo White. Each man was armed and wearing navy-blue uniform, body armour and helmet. The PCs and the sergeant carried Heckler & Koch repeater rifles, the Inspector had a Glock handgun in a shoulder holster. In addition, there were three men and one woman from the Bromersley station. The men, Crisp, Scrivens and Angel, were dressed in striped grey trousers, white shirts, waistcoats and dicky bows. Each man carried a crisply laundered serviette over his arm. The woman was Flora Carter, dressed in a plain blue skirt and white blouse with a long chain leading from her waistband to keys in her pocket.

Downstairs, DC Ahmed Ahaz was behind the reception desk in the Feathers Hotel. He was in his best dark blue suit, white shirt and tie. He was rubbing shoulders with two regular receptionists. He tried to look busy and act the part. Whenever a visitor came forward, Ahmed took a step backward and a genuine receptionist dealt with any inquiry.

Ahmed was there to monitor the arrival of Harrison, aka Mr MacDonald, Mickey 'the Loop', Thomas Johnson, the girl with the orange lipstick and any other crook that he might recognize from the photographs on the PNC.

At 12.30 p.m., a big man arrived at the reception desk in a Reid & Taylor suit. He was carrying a pigskin suitcase.

'Can I help you, sir?' one of the genuine receptionists, a woman called Jane, said.

'My name is MacDonald,' the man said.

Ahmed's ears pricked up. His heartbeat quickened. It certainly looked like Harrison. He hardly dare risk looking directly at the man. He pretended to be checking a bill.

'My secretary reserved a suite for me.'

'Yes, that's fine, Mr MacDonald. Everything is prepared for you. Suite 1 on the first floor. If you'd care to sign the book?' she said as she swivelled it round on the turntable.

The man put his suitcase down on the carpet. Then, as he brought his hands up to the counter, his coat sleeve fell back and Ahmed noticed a gold Cartier watch with a crocodile strap on his wrist.

The man signed the book, Jane banged a bell and said, 'If you need anything, Mr MacDonald, just pick up the phone in your room. The porter's coming.'

Harrison nodded, and turned away towards the body of the hotel. As he did so, Jane saw a short, miserable-looking little man who had been standing directly behind Harrison, with his hands in his pockets.

She thought he seemed strange. 'Can I help you, sir?' she said.

He reached down for the suitcase. 'No, I'm with him . . . Mr Donaldson,' he said.

His eyes half-closed except when he spoke. His voice made her hair stand up at the back of her neck. The colour drained from her face. He was oily and menacing . . . like a snake.

'There is a colour television in the room, isn't there?'

She gulped. 'Yes. Oh yes, sir,' she managed to say.

The man turned away and caught up with Harrison, who had been looking for a sign to the lifts.

Jane found a tissue and held it across her mouth.

A liveried young man appeared, and looked around the reception area, then up at Jane, who was holding out a key. He took the key, then she pointed at Harrison, but she couldn't speak.

The young man said, 'What room number?'

Jane turned away from him.

The porter's fists tightened. 'What's the flaming room number?'

Ahmed came to her rescue. 'Suite number 1,' he said.

The porter gawped at Ahmed. 'Well, where's the luggage, then?' he said.

Ahmed said, 'The other man with him has taken his case.'

The young man pulled an angry face, turned away and rushed in front of Harrison and the short man.

'This way, gentlemen, please,' he said.

As they went into the lift, Ahmed picked up the phone.

'There are two men on their way up now, sir,' he said. 'Harrison, who has signed in as J. MacDonald and party, and the other, who is only short, seems foreign, I expect he is Mickey "the loop".'

'Yep. That's them, Ahmed,' Angel said. He put the phone back in its cradle on the wall in the service room and turned round to the team.

'Harrison and Mickey are on their way up, so quiet, everybody, please.'

Angel then opened the door an inch and listened.

The lift doors whooshed.

'This way, gentlemen,' he heard a voice say.

It was followed by the rustle of clothes as the men ambled the few yards of the corridor from the lift to the main door of the suite. Then he heard the rattle of a key hitting wood, the sound of its withdrawal from the lock, the swish of the door opening, more rustling of clothes, and then the bang of it closing.

Angel closed the service door, turned to DI Waldo White and said, 'Right, that's the first two.'

'How many do you expect, Michael?' White said.

'There's Thomas Johnson and the girl. Four altogether. It would be a nice catch, if we can pull it off.'

'You've nothing on the girl?'

'No, but she might make a nice witness, Waldo. Excuse me.'

He'd seen DS Carter looking inside her handbag.

'Flora, do you happen to have any mascara . . . and a brush?'

'Mascara?' she said, smiling. '*You*, sir? Of course. Do you want some?' she said with a laugh.

Some of the FSU lads heard the exchange and grinned.

'Yes, please,' Angel said with a perfectly straight face.

The phone on the wall rang. He squeezed through to the place on the wall and took it out of its holster.

'Room service,' he managed to remember to say. But it was Ahmed. 'Yes, lad?'

'Thomas Johnson and that girl with the orange lipstick are on their way up, sir,' Ahmed said.

'Right, thank you.'

He replaced the phone, squeezed his way across to White and told him the news. Then he said, 'Quiet, everybody, please, while I open the door a minute.'

He listened through the tiny gap.

He heard them arrive in the lift, come round the corner, knock on the door, which opened and closed without any conversation. Then he closed the door.

'The four of them are in position.'

Angel rubbed his chin. After a while, he went over to the cupboard where the cutlery and pots were stored. He looked on the shelves at all the stuff that appeared on the hotel table. He frowned until he found himself looking at the cruets. He picked up a salt pot, looked at it. It had a silver lion, an anchor and the date letter 'S' in an italic font, so it was silver and hallmarked in Birmingham in 1970. He pressed it into the palm of his hand. He put it back, then he did the same with a pepper pot. He nodded and picked up another three identical pepper pots and dropped them into his pocket. Some of the FSU squad saw him and looked puzzled. He had seen them but said nothing and gently squeezed past them to get back to DI White.

'I hope we don't have to wait long,' White said.

Angel nodded. He gestured towards the phone and said, 'We only have to wait until they want something from room service, Waldo.'

'Michael,' White said. 'Suppose they don't ring?'

His heart fell into his boots. He rubbed his chin. Eventually he said, 'Well, we'd have to think of something else.'

At three o'clock that afternoon, a bell rang. Twelve eager faces in the first-floor hotel service room turned to the phone on the wall.

Angel took a deep breath, cleared his throat and picked up the phone. 'Room service. Can I help you?'

'I want a bottle of good whisky, bottle of Bacardi, bottle of lime juice, soda water, ice and four glasses straightaway.'

'Yes, sir,' Angel said. 'Anything else?'

'Yes. An assortment of sandwiches. A big assortment of sandwiches. For four. All right?'

'Thank you, sir,' Angel said. His stomach was like a hornet's nest that had been knocked over.

'What room number are you, sir?' he added, although he knew full well it was Mickey 'the loop' Zeiss speaking.

Angel heard him say away from the phone, 'He say what room number we are?'

'Suite 1,' a voice said.

'Suite 1,' Mickey 'the loop' Zeiss said.

'Right away, sir,' Angel said.

He cancelled the call, then dialled the number for reception and gave the details of the order to Ahmed to organize. 'As quick as they can, lad, please.'

He replaced the phone and Angel put the final touches to the plan. It began with Flora Carter.

She picked up a pile of clean towels and went out of the service-room door and down the corridor a little way to the door to Suite 1. She knocked on the door, waited for a reply and there was none. They must be in the sitting room. Relieved, she let herself in with a pass key. She was pleased to note that the door to the sitting room was closed although she could hear voices. She was making her way to the bathroom when she heard the toilet flush, the door opened and out came Mickey 'the loop'.

He blinked, staggered and shoved his right hand into his pocket when he saw her.

She stood by the door, gripping the towels, and froze.

He looked at her closely.

'What you want?' he said in that snake-like voice.

She breathed in and said, 'Excuse me, sir. I was just bringing you fresh towels. Sorry if I disturbed you.'

Mickey walked round her, still staring at her, looking her up and down and smiling.

Flora didn't like being stared at in such a way and for such a length of time.

She forced a smile and said, 'Excuse me,' and she went into the bathroom.

She heard an impatient voice from the sitting room call out, 'Mickey, come on. We're waiting for you.'

She heard him say, 'I'm coming. I'm coming,' and then the door to the sitting room closed.

She exchanged the towels there with the ones she was carrying and came out, being careful to leave the door into the corridor unlocked.

She walked the few steps back to the service room.

Angel let her in. 'Everything OK?'

'Yes. I bumped into Mickey "the loop" Zeiss,' Flora said. 'He's awful. Undresses you with his eyes.'

'He didn't suspect anything?'

'No, sir. The four of them are now in the sitting room.'

He nodded approvingly. He wanted them all in the sitting room. It was necessary for the plan to succeed. The plan had to succeed or there would be a bloodbath.

Angel said, 'So that the four of us act in unison when we are in there, I want you, Trevor, to arrest Mickey "the loop" Zeiss. He's only a small man but he's vicious and not easily subdued. Keep his hands out of his pockets. There is probably a gun in each. All right?'

'Yes, sir,' Crisp said.

'I want you, Ted, to take on Thomas Johnson. He's a big lump, probably not armed, but don't take any chances. The trouble is that Johnson knows me. I am hoping that he won't recognize me in this dress and in this context.'

'Right, sir,' Scrivens said.

'And you, Flora, I want you to take on the girl. Now, she's an entirely unknown quantity.'

Flora nodded.

'I'll take on Harrison. I'll go in first and I want you to line up behind me, with Flora at the back. Obviously you'll need to position yourself as close to your target as you can. I will try and take note of that before I give the signal.'

A single ping informed them that the dumb waiter had arrived with the order. Angel produced four small silver salvers from the cutlery cupboard and distributed the order of drinks and glasses fairly evenly across the trays.

The sandwiches were on a platter under a large silver cover. He would carry that in.

He quickly applied a small moustache to his face using Flora Carter's mascara brush, distributed the pepper pots from his pocket, one to each of the other three, and then they lined up as a procession. Angel took the front, then Crisp, then Scrivens and lastly, Flora Carter. They put the serviettes smartly over their right arms, and held the trays up high on their left hands.

'Remember, the cue is when I remove the silver cover off these sandwiches. All right?'

The three nodded.

Angel then opened the room service door, and out the four processed to the main door of Suite 1, while the eight FSU men led by DI White stealthily moved down the corridor a few yards to assemble outside the door to the bedroom.

When everybody was in position, White gave a thumbs-up, and Angel knocked on the main door.

Angel could hear voices but what they were saying was indistinct. He waited a little, then knocked louder.

'There's somebody at the door,' a voice said.

All went quiet. Angel's heart pounded like a Salvation Army drum.

Suddenly it was whisked open by Mickey 'the loop' Zeiss.

He looked up at Angel strangely. 'Yes?' he said.

In a voice like a theatrical butler, Angel said, 'Your refreshments, sir.'

Mickey grunted and opened the door widely.

Harrison said, 'Yes, come in, come in.'

The other three were seated in a semi-circle in front of a coffee table. The unoccupied chair nearest the door appeared to be Mickey's chair.

'May we serve you, sir?' Angel said.

Harrison hesitated, flashed his big teeth, shrugged and said, 'Why not?'

The team put the trays onto the coffee table, while eyeing up their targets and closing in on them. Crisp took the whisky bottle and began to open it, Scrivens took the Bacardi and opened that, and Flora took the lid off the ice bowl. Angel slowly edged up to Harrison, then glanced at the others, bent down, then lifted the cover with a flourish, and said, 'Your sandwiches, sir.'

At that moment, the four took the pepper pots out of their pockets and rammed the tops of them hard into the stomach of their personal targets.

'Don't move any of you or you will be shot,' Angel said in a loud voice. 'This is a police raid.'

Harrison glared at Angel and said, 'You frigging bastard.'

The girl screamed.

'It's bloody Angel,' Thomas Johnson said.

On cue, the eight FSU men dashed through the door from the bedroom, waving their Heckler & Koch rifles.

It was all over.

SIXTEEN

As Angel walked down the corridor at the police station the following morning, he received smiles and nods from almost everybody. Inspector Haydn Asquith from the uniformed side of the force was behind him. He caught him up and said, 'Morning, Michael. Congratulations. Hear you arrested the hatchet man and his gang yesterday. That's great stuff.'

'Well, *I* didn't arrest them. It was a team job, Haydn, and we had the FSU behind us.'

'I heard you got a bug fitted in the phone of one of them?'

'That's right. DS Carter did that.'

'Flora Carter?'

'That's right.'

'Huh. You're lucky getting brains and beauty on your team. All my female officers have to shave and wear size eight boots.'

Angel smiled. He reached his office. Ahmed was outside waiting for him, so he waved Haydn Asquith goodbye.

Ahmed had a bundle of newspapers under his arm. He was quite breathless and smiling from ear to ear.

'It's in all the papers, sir,' he said. 'Many of them on the front page. I told my mother that you'd arrested that gang and that I was there at the time.'

Angel smiled. Then his phone began to ring. 'Better take this call,' he said.

'Right, sir. I'll come back later,' Ahmed said.

He nodded, dashed into the office, reached out for the phone and said, 'Angel.'

It was the civilian switchboard operator. 'There's a man from Reuters news agency wants to interview you about the hatchet man arrest,' she said. 'I'd like to take this opportunity of congratulating you on that too, Inspector.'

'That's very kind, but it wasn't—'

'And there's been four earlier calls from different newspapers,' she said.

Angel rubbed his chin. He couldn't spend all day repeating what had happened. Everything that could be told had already been told. There was nothing new to report. But he mustn't seem to be rude or offhand. There were times when he needed their help and cooperation and occasionally a reporter had given him a useful tip-off.

'Would you please tell him that I am out and that you don't know when I'll be back?'

'Do you want me to say that to *all* the media?'

'Yes, please. But only today. The arrest will be history tomorrow.'

It was Saturday night, June 15th, the night of the Fancy-Dress Ball in the grand hall of Muick Castle. Everybody who thought they were somebody in Bromersley was there. Most were dressed in exceedingly interesting hired or home-made costumes.

In the big oval-shaped hall, there were lots of small tables and chairs arranged near the walls, to leave the centre for dancing. At one end of the hall was a six-piece orchestra, playing a waltz, and a few couples were taking full advantage of the occasion.

At the bottom of the grand staircase on a raised dais sat Lady Muick in fancy dress and wearing the fabulous diamond and emerald necklace. Next to her was Mrs Nancy

Mackenzie. On her right was the diminutive figure of Sir Rodney Stamp, looking as fierce as ever and holding a glass of something alcoholic which a young man kept exchanging for a fresh glass when necessary. Next to Sir Rodney was a different young woman from the last ball. She had a big bosom, long legs, was wearing very little and wearing it exceedingly well.

Angel was sitting at a table nearer the orchestra sipping a whisky. He was there as the 'Turkish Ambassador' looking quite imposing. His facial expression belied his unhappy embarrassment. He felt as if he had arrived at the wrong place on the wrong night in somebody else's clothes. Mary was sitting next to him, smiling and sipping an orange juice. She looked most gracious and beautiful as the 'Queen of Sheba.'

Angel kept glancing at the voluptuous girl next to Sir Rodney Stamp. For some reason he was unable to take his eyes off her, and it wasn't because of the square yards of young, lightly tanned skin she was displaying.

The hall was becoming busy. Couples of all ages, and a few young girls, were dancing together and filling the dance floor.

Lydia and Stewart Twelvetrees and Nadine Tinker eased their way through the throng and came up to Michael and Mary Angel. The ladies greeted each other and began to talk about the fancy-dress costumes of others and then about their own outfits.

Twelvetrees said, 'I see congratulations are in order, Michael.'

'Well, thank you, but it was a team thing, Stewart, and we were supported by the FSU.'

Twelvetrees grinned. 'It's refreshing to meet a modest copper.'

Angel was determined to change the subject. 'By the way,' he said. 'I haven't seen your father in a while; how is he?'

'He's fine, Michael. He couldn't come tonight. Mum tells me he is still working at the office. He has to pick up the threads of all the cases of Juliet Gregg, who is leaving them soon.'

'Ah, yes. The one who is going to be a judge.' He sipped the whisky and looked round the hall. It was filling up. 'Good turn-out tonight. Should do the charity some good.'

'I hope so,' Twelvetrees said. 'It's a very worthy cause.'

'Mmm. And I hope there isn't another attempt at the robbery of her ladyship's necklace.'

Twelvetrees grinned. 'Mrs Mackenzie kept you very busy that night.'

'She did indeed. When we received our tickets for tonight, I phoned her and asked her to be aware that her ladyship would be taking an unnecessary risk if she intended wearing it in public tonight. Mrs Mackenzie said that she had everything in hand, but I notice the old lady is still wearing the necklace.'

'You can't tell women what to do, Michael,' Twelvetrees said, 'especially old codgers like her.'

Angel smiled.

'Must move on, Michael,' Twelvetrees said. 'Excuse us.'

'Of course,' Angel said. 'Nice to see you.'

'And you.'

Twelvetrees turned away. 'Come along, girls,' he said, 'Lydia, Nadine, we mustn't monopolize Mr and Mrs Angel. It's time we were moving. 'Bye for now, Mary.'

Then Lydia Twelvetrees and Nadine Tinker smiled sweetly at Angel and Mary and followed Stewart through the crowd.

Angel and Mary resumed their seats. When the Twelvetrees party were safely out of earshot, Mary said, 'That was a very low-cut dress Lydia was wearing. I asked her who she had come as and she said Lady Gaga.'

Angel didn't know what reply she expected from him so he said nothing.

'Didn't you think so?' she said.

He rubbed his chin and then eventually said, 'Yes.'

A waitress came round carrying a tray of drinks. She didn't look too safe with the tray and the floor was getting rather crowded. Angel stood up to try to help her through. 'Excuse me,' he said several times and went ahead of her a few yards to clear the way. When he came back, he was frowning and shaking his head.

Mary noticed and said, 'What's the matter?'

'That waitress,' he said. 'She didn't say anything but she rattled as she walked.'

It was Mary's turn to frown. 'What do you mean, she rattled as she walked?'

'I've heard it before . . . in the station . . . many a time. She rattled.'

'What are you talking about?'

'If I'm not mistaken, she's carrying a pair of handcuffs.'

'Oh? So what? There's not a law against it, is there?'

'No,' he said. He pursed his lips, had a sip from the glass, then said, 'It's interesting though, isn't it?'

Mary's face eyes opened wide and her jaw dropped. 'Interesting?' she said. 'I can't find anything *interesting* about it.'

Angel sniffed. 'Well, why would a waitress carry a pair of handcuffs?'

'I have no idea, Michael. It's not important, is it?'

He shrugged.

The orchestra began to play the introduction to 'You are my Sunshine'.

Angel's eyes meandered round the room and inevitably wandered back to the dais and the half-dressed girl.

Eventually, he turned to Mary and said, 'Who is the new girl with Sir Rodney Stamp, then?'

'I've noticed you keep looking at her,' she said with a teasing pretence at being jealous.

Angel ignored the taunt. He was serious. 'Who is she? What is she?'

'All I know is that her name is Mandy and that she has come as a "belly dancer".'

His eyes flashed. 'A belly dancer, of course,' he said. 'A belly dancer. And what's her name? Mandy what?'

'I don't know, but I can find out. Why are you so interested?'

'My interest is purely professional, my little dove,' he said.

He sipped on the whisky.

Dancers whizzed past.

Then Angel's face changed. He half-closed his eyes, put the glass down and pursed his lips.

Mary recognized the look. He was in thinking mode. Something had triggered the change. It would be to do with work. It always was. He could be five minutes or five hours. And it was something to do with the girl Mandy. She looked up at the dais. To Mary she looked like a tart wearing a rather vulgar costume. She couldn't begin to imagine what impression the costume or lack of it had made on her husband.

Unexpectedly, there was a loud roll on the drums and a crash of cymbals. The lights went out and a spotlight showed up a young man in white tie and tails in front of the orchestra.

The Great Hall went silent and everybody stared in the direction of the stage.

Into a microphone, the young man said, 'Good evening ladies and gentlemen, and welcome to the Fancy-Dress Charity Ball in the Great Hall here in Muick Castle, graciously permitted by Lady Muick, and sponsored by Mrs Nancy Mackenzie. I am your MC for the evening. Will you please take your partners for a quickstep?'

Before the orchestra could begin, there was a loud scream from the opposite end of the hall. In the dark, everybody turned towards the disturbance. Those who were seated stood up.

In a commanding voice, a woman called out, 'Put the lights on.'

Angel recognized the voice. It belonged to Nancy Mackenzie.

'Close and man all the doors,' she said. 'Mr Kyle, are you in the hall?'

'I'm here,' a broad Scots voice said.

The hall doors all slammed shut.

'Please take over,' she said.

'Aye. I will that, Mrs Mackenzie.'

The lights went up.

Kyle jumped up onto the stage and went up to the microphone. 'Everybody please stay exactly where you are,' he said. 'Team A, please check the toilets.'

Angel saw that Lady Muick was on her feet, her fingers feeling round her neck, and calling, 'My necklace is gone. It has been stolen!'

Sir Rodney Stamp said, 'Where did you have it last?'

Mrs Mackenzie said in a loud voice, 'Mr Kyle, Lady Muick's emerald and diamond necklace is missing.'

'Right, ma'am,' Kyle said. Then he spoke into the microphone. 'Ladies and gentlemen, all the dining room and bar staff and myself here this evening are employed by the Lion Security Group commissioned by Lady Muick's insurance company. And I hope you will cooperate with us to recover her ladyship's necklace. All the doors to the castle are now closed and locked. Nobody will be allowed through them until the search is completed. The toilets are at this time being cleared and I regret access to them will not be allowed until they have been searched.

'You will soon find among you men and women with metal detectors. Would you please allow my staff to pass the detectors across your person and, in the case of you ladies, your handbags as well? When you have been scanned, if you will permit it, an ink stamp will be made on the back of your left hand. The detectors will not touch you or your clothing and will take only a few seconds per person. I apologize in advance for this action. Your agreement to it is purely voluntary. If anyone is unwilling to be searched or stamped in this way, please let me know by raising your hand and I will come to you. If anyone is seated, would you please stand but do not move your position. Would Team B please proceed.'

A dozen men and women in waiters' and waitresses' attire came forward to the patrons and waved the small, hand-held metal detectors systematically across their faces and all the way down to their feet both back and front, then stamped them with an ink star on the back of their hands.

Angel noticed a young, slight woman edging slowly away from the dais and weaving her way stealthily between the patrons towards the stage at the orchestra end of the room. It was Lydia Twelvetrees. She kept her head down and carefully watched the security people before making a move.

Angel saw her husband, Stewart, who was only five yards away from him. Stewart was standing next to Nadine. He was looking into the crowd. He seemed anxious. Lydia must have seen them. She changed direction and made straight for her husband and sister. They were pleased to be reunited and made a few whispered exchanges. Meanwhile the security team were making quick progress through the crowd. Those being checked were being asked to move to the east side of the room while the team worked in a more or less straight line westwards. Lydia Twelvetrees was only one or two away from being checked.

Angel noticed her face was as white as Strangeways' lavatory walls.

Suddenly she said, 'Oh, I feel faint, Stewart, I must sit down.'

Twelvetrees bit his lip. 'Can you not stand for two or three minutes more?' he said, his face reddening. 'It's us next, look.'

'No. No,' she said and she slumped down into a chair.

Nadine produced a glass of water. 'Here, Lydi darling, drink this.'

She brushed it away. 'I need to go to the powder room.'

Twelvetrees put up a hand.

Mr Kyle came rushing up to him. 'What's the matter, sir?'

Twelvetrees whispered, 'It's my wife . . . she needs to go to the powder room.'

Kyle said, 'Aye. That's all right, sir. Can she walk?'

'Oh yes,' Lydia said. 'I can walk.'

'Right, ma'am, wait there. I'll just get an escort for ye,' he said and dashed off.

Lydia looked up at her husband, her mouth and eyes wide open and her hands shaking. Stewart Twelvetrees held her hand and said, 'It'll be all right, darling. He's just gone to get help.'

Kyle returned with two security women. He said, 'These two ladies will look after you, missy. You'll be all right. Just do what they say, and you'll be all right.'

'Stewart, darling,' Lydia said, putting her arms out towards him.

'It'll be all right, darling,' Twelvetrees said.

'We'll be here, Lydi, waiting for you,' Nadine said.

The two women helped her to her feet and trooped off with Lydia between them.

The security team speedily checked Angel, Mary, Twelvetrees, Nadine Tinker and everybody else and asked them in turn to move to the east side of the hall. The check was completed in a few minutes. Then the team began searching the west side of the hall and suddenly a call went out, and a member of the team held his hand aloft. There was an interested murmuring through the patrons.

Kyle came running forward.

The man who had held up his hand pointed to something under a table a few yards away from where Angel and Mary had been sitting.

Kyle could be heard muttering something. Then he reached under the table and pulled out a glittering piece of jewellery. Then Kyle smiled widely and held it up to Mrs Mackenzie and Lady Muick.

He dashed across to the dais and handed it up to Mrs Mackenzie, who immediately passed it on to her ladyship.

Murmurs of pleasure ran throughout the hall. Even Sir Rodney Stamp managed a smile as he beamed at the half-clad young lady next to him.

Somebody started to clap, it quickly spread and the entire hall joined in and clapped enthusiastically.

Mrs Mackenzie rose to her feet and said, 'May I have your kind attention for just a moment, please. I won't hold up the dancing any longer. Clearly someone attempted to take Lady Muick's necklace. They failed. It has now been returned to her ladyship, and I simply want to thank everybody on behalf of the committee for patiently allowing the security company to do their job. Thank you. The matter is now closed. Mr MC, would you please ask the orchestra to play some music?'

She sat down.

The MC immediately made the announcement. 'Ladies and gentlemen, please take your partners for a quickstep.'

The orchestra began to play the introduction to 'In the Mood'.

Angel saw Lydia return unescorted through the doors that led to the powder room and toilets, which were now open and unsupervised. She was still pale and kept her eyes looking downward as she found her husband in the crowd.

Angel rubbed his chin for a few moments, then his eyes wandered away from her and up to the girl on the dais. After a few moments, he stood up and without saying anything to Mary, who was talking to somebody, he casually walked across the corner of the room and then stepped up onto the dais.

Mrs Mackenzie said, 'Good evening, Inspector. What can I do for you?'

'Do you think that I could take a look at the necklace?'

'I assure you that it's all right,' she said, 'except that the chain is broken at the back near the clasp.'

'Yes,' he said, 'that's what I would like to see.'

She went across to her ladyship. 'You know Inspector Angel?' Mrs Mackenzie said to Lady Muick.

The old lady looked at him vaguely and said, 'Yes. Good evening, Inspector.'

'Good evening, ma'am.'

Mrs Mackenzie said, 'He wants to look at your necklace. Where is it? You put it in its case, didn't you? Where's the case?'

She ferreted around in several bags at the feet of the old lady.

Sir Rodney Stamp looked across at him, wrinkled his nose, yawned, then turned away. Angel took the opportunity to look more closely at the sparsely dressed young woman next to him who had come as a belly dancer. He stared very interestedly at her slim, brown abdomen.

Mrs Mackenzie meanwhile had found the jewellery case and opened it for him to see the necklace. 'Tut, Inspector Angel,' she said with a flash of ill temper, 'do you want to see this necklace or not?'

'Oh yes, of course,' he said, turning back.

'It *is* the genuine article,' she said. 'It has not been substituted for paste or anything like that.'

'No, no, I don't expect it has. I was curious to see how it was actually taken from around her ladyship's neck. Ah, I see it is a clean cut. It was simply removed with a pair of snips, cutters or pliers. That's all I need to know, thank you.'

'Do you know who the thief is?' she said.

'No, Mrs Mackenzie, I regret that I *don't* know. But I hope to find out quite soon.'

When he returned to Mary, he found that she was not very pleased. 'What's the idea of making a fool of yourself like that, ogling that half-dressed girl up there on the dais? Half the room was looking at you.'

Angel shook his head. He frowned. 'Were they? I didn't notice.'

'And another thing, have we come here to dance or not?'

His head went up. He was listening to the music.

'It's all right,' she said. 'It *is* a waltz.'

'In that case, madam,' he said with an exaggerated flourish and a bow, 'would you care to accompany me in a bit of Terpsichore?'

She couldn't help but smile. He held out his arms and they swished off onto the busy dance floor.

They reached the far end of the room and were enjoying the dance, the orchestra, and looking at the varied costumes

— although Angel had spotted three Elvis Presleys and two Ann Widdecombes — when he saw Stewart and Lydia Twelvetrees and Nadine Tinker making for the exit. He blinked and pointed them out to Mary.

'They're leaving early,' he said.

'Could be Lydia's not very well,' Mary said.

'She's certainly very pale.'

'I wonder what's the matter?'

Angel shook his head.

SEVENTEEN

Stewart Twelvetrees drove the car up the drive to his house and stopped at the front door. The heat-sensitive lights flooded the whole area.

'Out you get, girls,' Twelvetrees said to sisters Lydia and Nadine, who were in the back.

The car doors opened.

'Do you want a hot drink to take up to bed, Stew?' Lydia said.

'No. Don't bother for me, darling. I'm just about bushed.'

'And I don't want anything, Lydi. I'm going straight up,' Nadine said.

The car doors slammed shut.

Twelvetrees drove up to the garage door and clicked on the remote. The door began to lift. He drove in. The door closed and he let himself in through the side door, which led into the hall. He locked the door, then checked the front door and went upstairs.

For fancy dress, he had been wearing a Victorian policeman's outfit. He undid the many buttons down the front of the long coat and took it off.

Lydia came in carrying a saucer with a glass of milk on it. She put it on the dressing table. She dragged the big hat off and scratched her scalp. 'I don't know who wore this before me, but I think they must have had fleas.'

Twelvetrees smiled. 'Had a good night, Lydia?'

'I've had better,' she said, throwing her bag onto the bed. 'I've been to places where I *wasn't* suspected of stealing the host's bloody necklace.'

'You were never suspected of stealing it.'

'You don't know what those butch so-called women said to me in the toilet,' she said as she began unpacking her bag.

Twelvetrees was now undressed to the waist. He went out through a door that led into the en-suite bathroom. 'What did they say to you?' he called. 'They didn't accuse you of stealing it, did they?'

'Not in so many words, but they wanted me to take *all* my clothes off. I took the coat off. That's all. I said I'm not taking anything else off. You can run that bloody machine over me if you want but you'll find sod all.'

'And did they?'

'Oh yes, and it triggered the damned thing. You should have seen the glee on their faces. But it was only the wire in the fastener on my suspender belt. Of course they were beaten then, so they packed their little toy up. But they wouldn't let me out of their sight — even in the lavatory cubicle.'

Twelvetrees came back into the bedroom a few minutes later dressed in his pyjamas and carrying a glass of water and a very flat tube of toothpaste. He put the glass on the bedside table and waved the empty tube at her and said, 'We're out of toothpaste, love. I can't squeeze any more out of this one.'

Lydia was almost ready for bed. 'I'll get some on Monday,' she said, then she dragged out a nightdress from under the pillow and went into the bathroom.

Twelvetrees dropped the toothpaste tube into the little wastepaper basket at the side of the dressing table. It landed on a used tissue, revealing something with a red handle. He bent down, pushed the tissue and the toothpaste tube to one side to reveal a small pair of cutters with red handles. He picked them out of the wastepaper basket, straightened up and looked at them. He frowned. He closed and opened them several times, then put them on the bedside table.

He pulled back the duvet and got into bed. He put his hands behind his head and leaned back against the bed head. He licked his bottom lip with the tip of his tongue. After a few seconds, he suddenly reached out for the red-handled cutters, looked at his fingernails and began to cut them. Then he swapped over and cut the nails on his other hand. He smiled, brushed away the clippings, replaced the cutters on the bedside table and returned his hands to the back of his head.

Lydia returned, rubbing some skincare into her hands. She looked at Twelvetrees and smiled sweetly. She turned out the light on her side, pulled back the duvet, got into bed and snuggled up to him. He put his arm round her.

'I suppose I did enjoy most of tonight, really,' she said. 'I was just being bitchy because those security people didn't believe me.'

Twelvetrees nodded.

She found an opening in his pyjama jacket and put her hand on his bare chest and made small, gentle, circular movements with her fingertips.

'Did you enjoy yourself, darling?' she said.

'It was nice seeing old friends,' he said.

'Mmm,' she murmured.

Then suddenly he said, 'Lydia, I want to ask you something.'

'Yes, darling?'

He turned back to the bedside table and picked up the cutters. 'I found these in the wastepaper bin. I wondered what they were doing there.'

Her eyes flashed. She quickly rolled away from him. 'What? They're nail cutters, what the hell do you think they are?' she said.

'I thought that's what they were. But what were they doing in the wastepaper bin, then?'

'What do you think? They're faulty so I threw them out.'

'Well, I've just cut *my* nails with them. They seem perfectly all right to me.'

'Well, they're *not* all right. They stick. They're bloody faulty. All right?'

His face creased. He closed the cutters and opened them several times. 'They work perfectly all right. Look. They don't stick at all.'

'Marvellous. You've repaired them. Big deal.'

She turned over to her own side, pulled the duvet up to her neck and said, 'Goodnight!'

Stewart Twelvetrees turned the light off on his side, settled down in the bed, closed his eyes; but he didn't get to sleep for several hours.

It was 8.28 a.m. on Monday when Angel arrived at his office. He looked down at his desk. That pot animal stared at him as it stood on top of the most enormous pile of paperwork; the monster made the pile underneath seem even worse.

He reached out, picked it up and glared at it. It glared back. He slammed it down. He rubbed his chin. He suddenly had an idea. He reached out for the phone and tapped in a number.

'Yes, sir?' Ahmed said.

'Come in here a minute, lad,' he said.

A few moments later Ahmed appeared.

'Ah yes, Ahmed,' he said. He carefully picked up the pot monster and said, 'Now, you like this . . . erm, unique figure, don't you, lad?'

Ahmed hesitated. 'Well, yes, sir. Why?'

'Do you think your mother would like this sort of thing? Is she into sheltering wildlife, save the whale, protect the . . . erm, pig and so on?'

Ahmed frowned. 'Oh *yes*, sir.'

'Well, I'd like to give you this.'

Ahmed's eyes lit up. 'Oh, *sir*,' he said, taking the ornament.

'You can give it to your mother, and tell her what a great lad she has for a son.'

'Oh *thank* you, sir. Can I take it now and put it away safe somewhere? I don't want to get it broken.'

'You can, lad. You can indeed.'

Ahmed dashed off with his trophy.

Angel sighed, then leaned back in his chair and smiled.

He pulled the pile of papers toward him and began to filter some of them out. Magazine subscriptions were being sought by the publishers of *Beekeepers' Weekly*, the *Planet Fortnightly*, *Cabbage Growers International*, *Natural Remedies for All* and *Kelp is Good for your Scalp*. He banished them all to the bin. He had just found another, *Navigation by the Stars*, when the phone rang.

It was Dr Mac.

'Is that you, Michael?' he said. 'Have you heard about Lydia Twelvetrees, young Stewart's wife?'

Angel's face changed. Mac sounded very solemn. 'No,' he said. 'What's happened?'

'She is *here* — well, her body is, for a post-mortem, which I have just finished.'

'Oh dear,' Angel said. He thought of her beauty and her sparkle being lost to the world, and she was so young. 'Whatever happened?'

'A witness said that she ran into the road behind a waiting bus and was hit by a furniture van. An ambulance was called, but it was too late. Her remains were sent here — I'm in the mortuary — for a post-mortem.'

'How awful, Mac,' Angel said. 'And how particularly unpleasant for you, knowing the woman . . . well, she was hardly a woman . . . how old was she? '

He thought about Stewart Twelvetrees, a bright, handsome young man, who would now become a widower at about thirty. Then he remembered her poor sister, Nadine. Whatever was to become of her? And Stewart's father, Marcus Twelvetrees, head of the CPS, would naturally be upset.

'Hardly twenty-four. Married about six years.'

'And what did you find, Mac? Is there anything criminal about her death?'

'Oh, no. She had some terrible injuries, but they were all the result of the impact with that van.'

'Is there anything I can do?'

'No, Michael. No. I thought you'd want to know, that's all.'

'Well, yes. I'll have to go to the funeral, and Mary will want to go.'

'Aye,' Mac said.

It was Monday, June 24th. It was dry and sunny, and the day of Lydia Twelvetrees' funeral.

Angel and Mary arrived at the Brambles on Old Horse Lane, a mile or so outside Bromersley town, at 11.30 a.m.

The Brambles was an old farmhouse with a large cobbled area in the front. There were already sixteen or seventeen cars parked there.

The front door was open and a young lady greeted them, offered them coffee and then suggested that they might care to join the other guests in the drawing room.

Angel and Mary, carrying their coffee, passed through the hallway and glanced up the aged wooden staircase at Lydia's old wooden rocking horse. It stood halfway up on a wide part of the staircase where it widened as it turned at right angles. It had been the only memory of her struggling years as a child, living with her mother and Nadine in a little terrace house on Canal Street.

Angel and Mary went into the drawing room, which was quite full. People were sitting and standing around, talking quietly among themselves. He saw many faces he knew and exchanged smiles and nods with them. Mrs Mackenzie gave them a gracious nod as if she was royalty. They found themselves standing next to Tina, the chubby receptionist at the CPS. She was next to the beautiful Juliet Gregg, who looked stunning in a little black lace number. Mary made some small talk with them both. Angel smiled, nodded politely as he sipped his coffee.

One of the mourners remarked on the fact that a hearse and several black limousines were arriving. Everybody looked through the big windows and watched the hearse reverse up to the front door. Shortly afterwards the undertaker and pall-bearers assembled in the hall and then went upstairs.

Moments later, Marcus Twelvetrees and his wife appeared and in a low voice he said, 'Thank you all for coming. I do hope the coffee is . . . to your liking. At least the sun is shining and it's not raining. Stewart and Nadine will be down directly. Our dear daughter-in-law's remains are in their bedroom . . . the undertaker's men have gone up to collect the coffin and bring it down to load it into the hearse. We will then be leaving for the church.'

Marcus Twelvetrees and his wife then turned and went into the hall, then Nadine Tinker came down the stairs followed by Stewart Twelvetrees. Nadine didn't look up at anybody. She stood next to Mrs Twelvetrees. Stewart didn't speak but he waved to everybody and took up a position next to his father.

Angel and Mary and most of the mourners in the drawing room drifted into the hall as they heard the murmurs of the funeral director on the landing instructing the pall-bearers.

The coffin appeared inch by inch and was maintained in a horizontal position throughout as the men slowly descended backwards. Then as they reached the turn in the stairs, the leading pall-bearer, who was holding the coffin chest high, backed into the head of Lydia's rocking horse and caught it with the heel of his shoe. There was the sound of a click and the head of the horse dropped down. Suddenly, gold chains, rings, brooches, glittering diamond rings, Victorian earrings with pearls, loose emeralds and rubies fell out onto the stairs.

There was a gasp from many of the mourners.

Angel saw it all and shook his head. It explained most of the robberies that had occurred in and around Bromersley over the past ten years or so.

Nobody said anything about it.

A car rug was thrown over the rocking horse and the spilled jewellery by Mr Twelvetrees Senior before he left for the church.

After the church service and the burial, most of the congregation returned for a light buffet lunch, then soon began to take their leave.

Twelvetrees Senior came up to Angel and said, 'Will you hang back, Inspector? We'll have to sort this rocking-horse business out.'

Angel said, 'Yes, of course.'

'Come in,' Angel said.

It was DS Taylor. 'Good morning, sir. We got comparison prints from the hairbrush on her dressing table.'

Angel said, 'And Lydia Twelvetrees' prints were the only prints on the jewellery, the gemstones and the rocking horse?'

Taylor nodded. 'Yes, sir. I'd say it was conclusive.'

Angel sighed. 'Aye, and she was working alone. Her sister said she knew nothing about the robberies nor about the rocking horse being hollow, and I believe her.'

'So it puts to bed all those jewellery robberies, sir.'

'It will be no comfort to the Twelvetrees family.'

'And you can't charge anybody.'

'No.'

There was a knock at the door.

'Come in,' Angel said.

It was Crisp, who was carrying a sheaf of papers.

Angel looked at him and what he was carrying and frowned. He turned to Taylor and said, 'Right, Don. Thank you. List and photograph that jewellery. We'll have to have a try at finding the owners. All right?'

'Right, sir,' Taylor said, then he went out.

Crisp watched Taylor leave and then he said, 'Was Lydia Twelvetrees the jewellery thief then, sir?'

'She was.'

Crisp shook his head in disbelief.

Angel was going to comment further, but changed his mind. 'Are you still on with those hospital records?' he said.

'Yes, sir. And I want to ask you a question about them. I've been on them ten days now.'

'I know, lad. It's time you'd finished them.'

'Well, there are thousands of them, sir, literally. It's like looking through a telephone directory except much worse, and they're not in alphabetical order. Your name — or the name Angel — has come up a few times. And my own name Crisp, I have seen, but I didn't bother checking it. I checked the name of the first Angel and it was to do with a man in North London paying for cosmetic surgery on his wife.'

'I've no relations there, as far as I know, but what about names of villains like Johnson, Harrison, Zeiss, or that landlord of the King George, Jack Vermont?'

'I thought you said it was a woman, sir.'

'I did . . . anyway, it's the surname that matters. We can't know the gender of the patient until we turn up the invoice. Look, lad, I feel it in my water that both Norman Robinson and Patrick Novak were most cruelly poisoned because they knew something about somebody that the murderer didn't want making public.'

'Blackmail, sir.'

'Exactly. And that that photograph of the baby is the key to the puzzle. And Trevor, that hospital is a private hospital, not your National Health. So it would have to be somebody with a few bob, who had a secret of some sort.'

'Even if the "few bob" came out of a racket of some sort, sir?'

'That's right.'

'And liked fruit gums?'

'That's right.'

Then Angel suddenly looked up at him and said, 'But just a minute, lad. When you came in you said you wanted to ask me a question.'

'Well, you've sort of answered it, sir. It was to ask you if you still wanted me to carry on searching the list?'

Angel's face went scarlet. 'Of course I want you to go on,' he roared. 'You have in your hands possibly the only lead to finding the murderer.'

EIGHTEEN

Angel picked up the phone and tapped in Ahmed's number. When he answered Angel said, 'Ahmed, find DS Carter and tell her I want her.'

A few minutes later DS Carter arrived.

'Ah, Flora,' he said. 'Come with me.'

He dashed up the corridor to the back exit of the station into the car park. Flora followed behind.

They got into the BMW and he drove it through the town.

She noticed he was particularly preoccupied and had nothing to say until he turned into Sheffield Road, then he opened up. 'You know a bit about plants, don't you, Flora?' he said.

'A bit, sir. Not much. Why?' she said.

'You know what monkshood looks like, don't you?'

'Oh yes, sir.'

'Well, I'm going to drive around the posh parts of the town and suburbs, and I want you to take a note of the gardens where you see monkshood growing. And when you do, shout up.'

She thought it was a bit strange. Of course, she knew the significance of monkshood to the Robinson/Novak murders, but she could easily do that job on her own and presumably the inspector could easily have done it without her. And besides all that . . .

'Don't you think it's rather a long shot, sir?' she said.

Angel's body tensed up. The BMW screeched to a stop.

Carter was expecting a vehicle to run into their rear. She looked round. There was nothing close behind.

She looked at him. He had his eyes closed. He opened them, looked back at her and through tight lips he said, 'Of course it's a *long* shot. What else have we got?'

Before she had chance to answer he said, 'I'll tell you, Flora. We've got two men with only half their clothes on, in their hotel bedrooms, cruelly poisoned with monkshood. We've got a solitary fruit gum on the floor by each of the beds, the photograph of a baby with a date on the back, a bunch of lilies bought from a shop that subsequently was fired by an arsonist. And . . . and . . . and that's about all I can think of.'

She stared at him with her mouth open.

But before she could reply he said, 'And talking about long shots, I've got Trevor Crisp wading through thousands of names of patients who were at that hospital in Norfolk since 2003, in the hope that he comes across the name of somebody connected with the case. That might be a longer shot than looking for local growers of monkshood! So I *am* backing long shots, Flora. What would *you* do?'

'I don't quite know, sir, but I do know there's no need for you to chauffeur *me* round. I am perfectly capable of finding gardens in and around the town that have monkshood in them, and then tripping off to the council tax office to find the owners of the gardens. And I'm sure that you *know* that.'

His lips tightened back against his teeth. 'I *do* know that,' he said. 'The trouble is, Flora, I'm running out of lines of inquiry. I am getting quite desperate. I'm on edge in case I can't solve this damned case.'

'You've always succeeded before, sir. Why do you think you won't solve this one?'

'Doors are closing, Flora . . . time is going on . . . I can't explain.'

'We'll get there, sir.'

Angel sighed. 'Maybe. Look, I'm sure you'd rather do this on your own.'

He reached forward, put the car in gear and the BMW set off again. 'I'll take you back to the station,' he said evenly.

He pulled into his parking space near the rear entrance to the station. He stayed in the car as she got out and went to her own car. Angel watched her. She was soon behind the wheel of the Ford and driving out of the yard.

Even on that short journey round Bromersley, something had occurred to him. Monkshood wouldn't be grown in the back streets. You wouldn't find monkshood in Canal Street or in terraced rows that didn't have gardens. The murderer would be relatively well off. At least he or she would live in a house with a garden. And he or she must have had access and privacy to a kitchen or scullery or similar to prepare the poison. And it still seemed logical (thinking back to the oriental lilies in Robinson's hotel room) that the murderer was a woman.

He thought he was part of the way there to solving the murder. He was looking for a well-to-do woman. Someone who was masterful and strong-willed. A woman who had something to hide.

An idea occurred to him. He started up the engine and put the car in gear. He went off to the Northern Bank and made some inquiries. He was in there half an hour. When he came out, he was much more settled. His breathing was steady and even. He looked happier and more content than he had for a week or more.

He got in the BMW and returned to the station. When he reached his office, he picked up the phone and tapped in a number.

A voice said, 'DS Carter.'

'Ah, Flora. How's it going?'

'Oh, hello, sir. There are loads of people with monkshood in their gardens up here.'

'Where are you?'

'High Bromersley. There's Lady Muick's castle gardens, Mrs Mackenzie, Sir Rodney Stamp and Mrs Truelove, widow of old Mr Enoch.'

Angel smiled. 'Great stuff.'

After a refreshing evening cutting the lawn and thinking things through, Angel arrived at his office full of optimism and go.

It was 8.28 a.m. Wednesday, June 26th.

He picked up the phone and tapped in a single digit for SOCO.

'DS Taylor.'

'Ah, Don. Later this morning, I want you to be prepared to go to Dr Kaye, or any JP of course, to get a warrant to make an arrest for murder and a warrant to search the subject's premises. In particular, I will want you to find those two tumblers that match the marks on the bedside table and the white porcelain shelf. And if you find them, I want you to phone me immediately, on my mobile. All right?'

He made two other urgent phone calls and then went out into the street, and walked next door to the Crown Prosecution Service.

'Good morning, Inspector,' Tina, the chubby receptionist, said. 'What can I do for you? I'm afraid Mr Twelvetrees is not yet back from compassionate leave.'

Angel frowned. 'Oh?'

Tina said, 'Miss Gregg's in, if you would like to consult her. Although she is leaving on Friday so . . .'

Angel nodded, thoughtfully. 'I know. Well, yes please, I would like to see her.'

Tina plugged in her headset. 'There's Inspector Angel. He really wanted Mr Twelvetrees, but . . . right, Miss Gregg.'

Tina replaced the phone, looked up at Angel and said, 'She says that's all right.' She pointed to a door. 'Please go straight in.'

Angel nodded. He went up to the door, knocked and opened it.

The beautiful Miss Gregg beamed up at him from her desk and indicated a chair opposite her. 'Please sit down, Inspector. I hope that you and your lovely wife survived yesterday's funeral, and have overcome the amazing revelation of all that jewellery. I assume you have come to ask about the legal position of the police in establishing the ownership of the various pieces?'

'No,' Angel said. 'We can deal with that, Miss Gregg. No, it's about something much more serious.'

'Oh yes?' she said.

'Yes. Yesterday afternoon, I went to the Northern Bank. I went there to inquire if anybody in the last week or so had withdrawn a large amount of cash and then repaid it soon afterwards.'

Her face creased. 'I don't understand your train of thought, Inspector.'

'You will, Miss Gregg, you will. You withdrew £10,000 at three o'clock on Wednesday the 5th of June and repaid it the next morning at 9.45 a.m. Would you like to tell me why?'

Her neck stretched upwards. The muscles round her small mouth tightened. Her eyes stood out like cherries on stalks. 'No. I would not *like* to tell you why, Inspector. It's an impertinent question, but, nevertheless, I *will* tell you. I had seen a car advertised in a paper. I thought I might buy it. The vendor would only accept cash. But when I got more details, it wasn't the car I thought it was, so I changed my mind and returned the money to the bank.'

Angel shook his head. 'It wasn't to give to Patrick Novak to put him at ease, was it?'

She frowned. 'Who was Patrick Novak?'

'You correctly used the past tense, Miss Gregg, because you know exactly who he was. He was the porter at Coalsden Cottage Hospital in Norfolk. He was setting himself up to blackmail you for the murder of your ex-boyfriend, Norman Robinson. And don't ask who Norman Robinson was. He was the father of your baby born in May 2002, when you were only seventeen.'

Her face went scarlet. Her mouth dropped open. 'This is absolute nonsense.'

'Is it? Well, where were you on the evenings of Sunday, June 2nd, and Wednesday, June 5th?'

'At home, I suppose. I can't remember.'

'Who with?'

'Nobody. I believe that you know that I live on my own.'

'I'll tell you where you were on Sunday, Miss Gregg. You were in Norman Robinson's room in the Feathers, seducing him . . . dancing in a belly dancer's costume with a red fruit gum stuck in your navel, to represent a ruby. You'd taken two glasses and a bottle of red wine doctored with the juice of the monkshood flower. You got him worked up into such a state that he would have agreed to anything, and after a glass of that mixed with wine, it was all over.'

'Have you got proof of this? Have you got CCTV of this? It's well known that the Feathers has CCTV all over the place. If I had been there, the cameras would most certainly have recorded my presence.'

'If you had entered and left by the back door, the door the staff use, and walked up the steps to the first floor instead of taking the lift, you would have avoided all the cameras. I discovered that when I used that exit to avoid a gathering of media in the reception area a few days ago.'

She carried on as if he hadn't said a word. 'But I would imagine in a hotel of that standing, that the back door would always be locked, and only unlocked in response to a bell or a signal of some sort.'

'That is quite right, Miss Gregg. You would know all about it. It's a Yale lock. You can't get in without somebody admitting you, but you *can* get out. That's why you needed an accomplice to let you in. It was easy for me to work out his identity. You had recently got a man released, a man who had a record a mile long. Thomas Johnson. And *you*, supposed to be prosecuting on behalf of the police! You had all his details. His address, phone number and so on. You set it up from this office, no doubt. We have a record of the date and time he phoned you here. And he was actually in the hotel bar drinking that evening. You had bribed him to let you in by the back door at a prearranged time.'

'Ridiculous. Has Johnson told you this story?'

'No, but when you are charged with murder, and he realizes that he might be charged as an accomplice, I think he will cough easily enough.'

'That's pure invention, Inspector. Why on earth would I want to murder anybody?'

'Ambition. Everybody knows that you hope to be a judge in a very few years. Any scandal, such as having a baby with a tearaway before the legal age, would have very much put you at a disadvantage.'

'You can't prove this.'

'We'll see. And that brings me to the evening of Wednesday, June 5th. Where were you that night?'

She pulled a sour face and shrugged.

'At home, I expect. On your own?' Angel said.

She didn't reply.

'That was the evening that Patrick Novak was poisoned in the George hotel. Novak was a very nosey hospital porter, in a posh, Norfolk private hospital, where all the patients were either exceedingly rich or had need to keep their medical situation confidential. Everybody knows that your parents had great plans for you, and it must have come as a mighty blow to them when you became pregnant at seventeen especially to a penniless seventeen-year-old layabout. They must have had a bob or two to be able to afford to send you away to that private hospital in the middle of nowhere for your delivery. At this time, Patrick Novak was quietly feathering his nest, taking secret and illicit photographs of patients and their visitors, listening at keyholes, noting addresses and so on, to use, where possible, in situations that might arise. So when he read in the papers that Norman Robinson had died in that ghastly way, he put two and two together and considered that you were a ripe candidate for blackmail. So he contacted you and you repeated the dose as before. It was even easier for you. As Patrick Novak stayed in the George hotel, where there was no CCTV, you didn't need an accomplice.'

'And do you expect a jury to believe this . . . this fairy story?'

'Absolutely, Miss Gregg. Because I can already prove most of it, and additional evidence is coming in all the time.'

'You really believe that I would lower myself to put on a dancer's costume . . . and . . . and perform for anybody, with a fruit gum in my navel?'

'Oh, yes. I also believe that you poured petrol into Enoch Truelove's shop and set fire to it in the certain knowledge that it would also burn out the fancy-dress-hire business on the floor above and thereby consume in the flames the woman's hire book, receipt book and anything else that would show that you hired a belly dancer's costume over that critical period. The tragic part of it was that old man Truelove lost his life trying to save his little greengrocer's shop from ruin.'

'You can't prove that, either.'

'I'm working on it. That's three men you have killed. I hope you are pleased with yourself.'

Angel's remote rang. He reached down into his pocket and opened it up. 'Angel,' he said. 'Yes, Don. Go ahead.'

As the caller spoke, Angel listened to him but had his eyes on Juliet Gregg. She was trying to look calm, ordered and superior.

'Thank you, Don. Goodbye.' He closed the phone and put it in his pocket.

'That was SOCO. We have a warrant to search your house. He is there now, and he reports that he has found two glass tumblers on your sideboard that exactly match the marks made by the two tumblers that had held poison and were present in both Norman Robinson's and Patrick Novak's rooms at their respective hotels.'

'That's impossible. And how dare you enter my house? If you have done any damage you will pay for it.'

'He also said that in the wild-flower area of your very big garden there are more than sixty plants of monkshood.'

She was breathing very deeply and trying to look unconcerned.

Angel's phone rang again. 'Excuse me,' he said to her as he answered it. 'Angel,' he said. 'Yes, Trevor? Right. Give me the details.'

Angel quickly took out his notebook and pen, and wrote as he listened.

'Right,' he said. 'Right. Got that . . . Right, goodbye.' He replaced the phone and turned to back to Juliet Gregg.

'And that was one of my sergeants to tell me that he has found the record which shows you were admitted to Coalsden Hospital on April 30th 2002, that you had a caesarean section on May 2nd and that a baby boy was delivered weighing 4 lbs 6 oz and that, sadly, the baby died a week later from breathing complications and pneumonia.'

Juliet Gregg's face turned to stone. 'What has happened to everybody? That hospital was supposed to offer a completely private and confidential service. Can nobody do the job they are supposed to do?'

Angel stood up.

'I shall deny everything,' she said. 'You're not going to get an easy ride.'

Angel opened his coat to reveal a microphone clipped to his coat and a thin cable that disappeared round his back to his hip pocket. 'It's all recorded here,' he said.

She laughed loudly in an exaggerated, mocking way. 'But you can't use recordings in court, Angel,' she said. 'I would have thought you would have known that.'

'It has also been transmitted to my sergeant, who should be in your reception area.' He looked across at the office door, and in a quiet voice said, 'Come in, Sergeant.'

The door opened and Flora Carter came in, taking off the headset and patting down her hair.

Juliet Gregg noisily sucked in a lungful of air. 'No,' she said, staring at the sergeant in disbelief.

'Did you get all that, Flora?' Angel said.

'Yes, sir.'

Juliet Gregg slowly stood up and continued to stare at the sergeant.

'Cuff her,' Angel said.

Flora took a pair of handcuffs out of her pocket, crossed the room to the young barrister and said, 'Miss Gregg, put your hands behind your back, please.'

Juliet Gregg screamed out, 'No! No!! No!!!'

There was a mighty tussle, but between them, Angel and Flora Carter soon managed to get the handcuffs on her.

Then Flora said, 'Juliet Gregg, I am arresting you on suspicion of murder. You do not have to say anything . . .'

Everybody in the station was both shocked and excited about the arrest of Juliet Gregg and congratulated Angel and the rest of the team.

Later that day, Ahmed came into Angel's office and said, 'Can I ask you a question, sir?'

Angel peered at him. ''Course you can, lad.'

'Well, what I don't understand is what first put you on to her, sir. I mean, she was ostensibly a pillar of respectability, wasn't she?'

He nodded. 'Indeed she was. Well, Ahmed, it was a couple of days back when I realized that the murderer must be someone in the know about forensics, because the murderer on each occasion took the tumblers as well as the poisoned wine away with them after each murder. He or she knew that the glass tumblers that had held poison in them could have told SOCO such a lot.'

Ahmed sat down and looked into Angel's eyes.

'I began to suspect old Marcus Twelvetrees,' Angel said, 'until I found out that the buying of the oriental lilies by Norman Robinson for his girlfriend had the ring of truth about it, because indeed, Robinson's pockets showed that he hadn't a bean, and dear old Enoch Truelove had said that Robinson hadn't quite sufficient money on him to be able to pay the full price. Then, of course, I realized the murderer must be a woman. Well then, there was only one woman in the CPS it could be, and that was Juliet Gregg.'

Ahmed nodded and smiled.

'Thereafter, I don't know how the mind works,' Angel said. 'I just know that when you've eliminated everything it couldn't be, you arrive at what it has to be and build on that. Which is what I did.'

'Wow,' Ahmed said with a big grin.

Angel smiled.

Angel closed the back door, locked it and looked round for Mary. Then he heard her running downstairs.

He went to the fridge and took out a can of German beer and a tumbler from the cupboard.

'Hello, darling,' she said. 'And congratulations.'

She put her arms round him. He reciprocated while still holding onto the can and the glass. They kissed.

'What's that for?' he said with a smile.

'Can't I kiss my husband if I want to?'

'Of course!' he said. 'Anytime. All the time.'

They both smiled.

'And congratulations on solving the case,' Mary said.

He stopped pouring the beer, frowned and said, 'How do you know that?'

'I would never have guessed it was Juliet Gregg. I always thought she was, erm . . . erm . . . too posh.'

'Nobody's too posh, sweetheart. But how did you know?' he said.

'You see. You're not the only detective in the house. Actually, Mrs Mackenzie has been on the phone to enrol me into assisting at the hospital library and she told me. She was amazed. She had been told by Mrs Dickens, who is a big noise in the WVS. She could hardly believe it. But it was her daughter, Tina Dickens, who works at the Criminal Prosecution Service, had rung her up and told her.'

'I see,' he said taking his first sip of the beer. Then he said, 'Any post?'

Mary smiled. 'Well, erm . . . yes. A present.'

He could see that there was something mischievous about her smile.

'Well, what is it, then?' he said.

'It's on the sideboard.'

His face changed.

He put down the beer and went into the sitting room. There was a long old sideboard against the wall as you walked in. At the near end was where the post, telephone messages and the like were usually to be found.

There was a small brown cardboard box addressed to Mr and Mrs Angel, with a customs declaration label stuck on the top and down one side. The box flaps were open and straw was sticking out of the top. He looked inside it and saw something shiny, a dirty brown and dark green. He frowned. There was a card with it. He snatched up the card. It read:

Dear Mary and Michael — Knowing how much you loved the porcelain ornament, we got you another, so that you can put one each end of the mantelshelf. Back on Friday.

Your loving neighbours,

Ken and Libby Copley. XX

Angel ran his hand through his hair.

THE END

ALSO BY ROGER SILVERWOOD

YORKSHIRE MURDER MYSTERIES

Book 1: THE MISSING NURSE
Book 2: THE MISSING WIFE
Book 3: THE MAN IN THE PINK SUIT
Book 4: THE MORALS OF A MURDERER
Book 5: THE AUCTION MURDERS
Book 6: THE MISSING KILLER
Book 7: THE UMBRELLA MURDERS
Book 8: THE MISSING MILLIONAIRE
Book 9: THE MISSING THIEF
Book 10: FIND THE LADY
Book 11: THE MISSING MODEL
Book 12: MURDER IN BARE FEET
Book 13: THE MISSING HUSBAND
Book 14: THE CUCKOO CLOCK MURDERS
Book 15: SHRINE TO MURDER
Book 16: THE SNUFFBOX MURDERS
Book 17: THE DOG COLLAR MURDERS
Book 18: THE CHESHIRE CAT MURDERS
Book 19: THE DIAMOND ROSARY MURDERS
Book 20: THIRTEEN STEPS TO MURDER
Book 21: THE FRUIT GUM MURDERS

Thank you for reading this book. If you enjoyed it please leave feedback on Amazon or Goodreads, and if there is anything we missed or you have a question about, then please get in touch. The author and publishing team appreciate your feedback and time reading this book.

We're very grateful to eagle-eyed readers who take the time to contact us. Please send any errors you find to corrections@joffebooks.com. We'll get them fixed ASAP.

Printed in Great Britain
by Amazon

52549813R00121